Drama High, Vol. 4
FRENEMIES

Drama High, Vol. 4
FRENEMIES

L. Divine

Dafina Books for Young Readers
KENSINGTON PUBLISHING CORP.
http://www.kensingtonbooks.com

DAFINA BOOKS are published by

Kensington Publishing Corp.
850 Third Avenue
New York, NY 10022

All Kensington titles, imprints and distributed lines are available at special quantity discounts for bulk purchases for sales promotion, premiums, fund-raising, educational or institutional use.

Special book excerpts or customized printings can also be created to fit specific needs. For details, write or phone the office of the Kensington Special Sales Manager: Kensington Publishing Corp., 850 Third Avenue, New York, NY 10022. Attn. Special Sales Department. Phone: 1-800-221-2647.

Dafina Books and the Dafina logo Reg. U.S. Pat. & TM Off.

ISBN-13: 978-0-7582-2532-0
ISBN-10: 0-7582-2532-6

First Kensington Trade Paperback Printing: January 2008
10   9   8   7   6   5   4   3   2

Printed in the United States of America

Acknowledgments

To my godfather, Baba Kofi A. Zannu Medahochi, who made transition during the completion of this novel; I am forever grateful for our time together. To my grandfather, Roger Harvey; to my uncle, Bryan Harvey who was more like a brother to me and the inspiration for the character. To my daddy, Claiborne Logan; to my step-daddy, Ricky Haskin; to Rashad Wilson, my oldest and truest friend; to Joshua Johnson, I wish you were still here to walk this path. To Larry Williams, Jewel Holloway, T.J. Desch, Baba Kwame Kalimara, Ras Markus, Ras Cello, Ras Prophet and the men of Eso Won books, thank you for your balancing energies.

And, to my readers, thank you for loving Jayd's path. To my students, all who knew and loved my class no matter the grade level, thank you for making me a better person on a daily basis. Without the experience teaching each student who came into my life allowed me, I would not be the woman I am today.

~Ase~

Prologue

"*Sometimes the people you think are your friends can be worse than enemies,*" *my mom says. I can hear her voice, but I can't see a thing. I feel suspended in time, like I'm in between the dream world and reality.*

"*Yeah, Mom. I feel you.*" *Did I say that aloud or in my head?*

"*They pretend to be your friend, while all the while, they really want more. They either want to feed off your popularity, talent, cookies, anything you've got to give. Whatever they think they can have, they will take.*"

This feels too real to be just a dream.

"*Remember, Jayd, lust takes, and love gives. And, I'm not talking about material things. Friends give their true selves to you. Frenemies, on the other hand, pretend to give until you start reciprocating. Then the giving turns into taking. And those are not friends. Those people are leaches. And, like all leaches, they must be eliminated in order for you to thrive.*"

For the second time since falling asleep last night, I sit straight up in my bed, breathing hard and sweating like I just ran a mile. Good thing I shower in the morning. Damn, what was that? It wasn't really a dream. It was more like a psychic conversation between me and my mom. I wonder if she did that on purpose.

My mom being able to read my mind really freaks me out still. She says she can get only in my head. I wonder how long she's been able to read my thoughts. Now she's sneaking into my dreams. Man, this is getting to be a bit much for a sistah. But, like my mom said, it comes with the territory of being a Williams woman, just like our never-ending drama.

"Jayd, wake up, girl. You're already five minutes late," Mama says without moving from her comfortable position in the bed across from mine. How she knows what time it is without looking, I'll never know. But I know she's right. I can hear Bryan stirring around in the kitchen, so I know it must be past time for me to get up. As I stumble out of my twin-size bed to retrieve my outfit for the day from the back of the bedroom door, I accidentally step on the rhinestone sandals Jeremy bought me sticking out from underneath my bed.

"Remember your mother's words, Jayd," Mama says, making me recall the dream I just snapped out of. As if it isn't bad enough I have Mama in my head, now my mom has crept her way in, too. What the hell?

~ 1 ~
Just Friends

"You, you got what I need/
But you say he's just a friend."

—BIZ MARKIE

After both Rah's surprise kiss yesterday afternoon and my first dream last night about Jeremy being Tania's baby-daddy, I'm even more confused about what to do with Rah and Jeremy. I can't front, Rah's kiss is still making me tingle, and I have to see Jeremy this morning. How can I look Jeremy in the face after what I did? Well, technically, what Rah did. But I could have stopped him if I really wanted to.

"Jayd, get out the bathroom. I need to go, now," my cousin Jay says, snapping me back into my morning routine. My cornrows are shiny from the mint shea butter Mama and I made last night. Mama supplies most of the beauty products for Netta's Never Nappy Beauty Shop: hair oil, sprays, lotions, soaps, essential oils, you name it. If it can be made, Mama can make it. And it'll be ten times better than anything you can buy at the beauty supply.

"Give me one more minute and then the bathroom's all yours," I say, packing my toiletries into my bath towel before taking one more look in the mirror. My yellow *Africa 1* T-shirt goes perfectly with my complexion, making my spirits lift. I love wearing bright colors. They make me feel good, despite whatever shit my environment may be throwing my way at the time.

"I don't have a minute, girl. Get out now!" Jay can be such a drama queen sometimes, I swear.

"Go around back and let it out. You a dude," I say as I continue to primp in the mirror. My uncles and Jay—probably Daddy, too—have all taken a piss out back before, either out of necessity or some sort of male bonding thing. It ain't nothing new to him.

"It ain't like that Jayd," Jay says, almost groaning. I guess I better let him in. Man, I miss the semiprivacy of my mom's house on the weekends. At least I don't have to share the bathroom with a bunch of men while I'm there. But it's only Monday, which means I have a entire week before I get some privacy again.

After returning my bathroom necessities to one of my three garbage bags turned dresser drawers in Daddy's room, I head to the kitchen to find Bryan eating breakfast and ready to go to work up the street at Miracle Market. He didn't get in until hella late last night, and I'm surprised to see him up and alert, even though his eyes are beet red.

"Hey, Jayd," Bryan says in between mouthfuls of cornflakes. I'm sure it's his second or third bowl. Early-morning munchies can do that to a brotha.

"What's up? Glad you made it home this morning," I say, grabbing a banana from the kitchen counter, heading into the dining room to retrieve my backpack and put on my sandals before heading out the door. I pull my sweater off the back off the chair where my purse is sitting and slip it on, even though it's going to be a warm day. It's October, and the weather is finally changing. And I'm sure it'll be even cooler once I get to Redondo Beach.

"Don't hate because Mama keeps you on lockdown, Blackerella. It's just part of being a girl," he says, thinking his little joke is funny. But it's not, and I'm tired of the double standard around here. If I'm supposed to be from a long line of powerful women, how come it seems we have so many limitations?

"Whatever," I say, tired of this argument. "I got to go before I miss my bus." I open the heavy door before tackling with the security gate. The wrought iron has been bent for years, making it hard to open.

"Wait up. I'll walk with you," Bryan says as he steps in front of me to open the gate in one quick motion. "Upper-body strength: another perk of being a man." As he steps back into the kitchen to grab his bag, I step outside on the front porch and take in a breath of fresh morning air. I love this time of the morning. Everything feels clean before the dew melts. Bryan slides his black bag over his head, barely missing his dreads.

"When you gone twist your hair up?" I ask. He looks like a poodle before it gets cut. And his hair's growing fast.

"As soon as I find somebody I can trust to twist it up for me," he says, nudging me as we walk down the street toward Alondra Boulevard. He's been trying to get me to do his hair for a while now. But I ain't looking forward to the charity work.

"You know a sistah don't work for free," I say, nudging him back but harder.

"How you gone make a nigga pay and we blood?" he says, looking genuinely hurt.

"How you gone expect something for free and we blood?" I say, mimicking his pitch perfectly. Bryan is more like a brother to me, and I love him the most out of all my uncles. But he's cheap, just like KJ. Maybe that's why they can hang. As if he's in my head, too, Bryan asks me about the dudes in my life.

"So, how's the White boy? I still can't believe you picked him over KJ," he says, sounding as confused as I feel.

"He's cool," I say, looking down at my yellow Bebe sandals. The shiny rhinestones shimmer in the morning sun,
making me remember what Rah said about dudes buying me
things. Between his warning at Homecoming and my mom's
warning in my dream, I'm starting to wonder about Jeremy's
true intentions.

"All right, what's wrong?" Bryan says, knowing I'm not telling the whole truth. Damn, he's intuitive for a dude.

"Well, Rah kinda came back into the picture recently," I
say, not wanting to tell him everything that happened. He
and Rah used to hang out, but not as much as he and KJ do.
Rah was all about spending time with me when he came
over, which was pretty much every day when we were together. It was whom he hung with after he left my house that
was the problem.

"Rah? What's that nigga up to? Him and Nigel still hanging
tight?" he asks.

"Yeah, Nigel goes to South Bay now," I say. I still can't believe it myself. How did my world get so small?

"Fo sho? That's some good shit right there. Now I won't
be so worried about your ass," he says, pushing me off the
curb as we approach Miracle Market.

"Glad my social life meets your approval," I say, a little
saltier than necessary. But this male bonding shit really gets
on my nerves sometimes.

"What's got your panties all up in a bunch?" he says, taking out a spliff and lighting it right in front of the store. Bryan
has no fear.

"Without getting too detailed, Rah says he just wants to be
friends, but I don't think he's telling the whole truth," I say,
leaving out the juicy kiss he planted on me.

"He's probably not, Jayd, and you know that. So what's
the problem?"

"The problem is I just got into a new relationship and there's already so much drama."

"Well, maybe it's the universe's way of telling you to make a different choice." If street philosophy were a major in college, Bryan would have a PhD in the shit.

"Oh, here you go. You need to apply for a job as a therapist or something and stop wasting your time working at the liquor store," I say as I walk away from his cannabis cloud toward the bus stop on the corner.

"No, thanks. I like my life just the way it is," Bryan says as he takes one last draw before putting it out and back into his bag, ready for work. "Can you say the same thing?"

As the bus pulls up to take me to my first stop in Gardena, I can't help but think about what Bryan just said. What if all this chaos in my relationship with Jeremy is telling me to make a different choice? Then what do I do?

After last week's Homecoming hype, I'm looking forward to a normal day at school. Nellie gets to sport her new crown around campus all day, and I'm glad for my girl. With the lunch procession of the Homecoming court taking up all her time, we probably won't get to chill too much today. Even though her head's still in the clouds, I'm glad she's coming down a little.

I can't stop thinking about my dream last night. And from my experiences, they usually come true in one way or another. I wonder if Tania really is pregnant with Jeremy's child. Wouldn't that be some shit? Young Middle Eastern girls getting married ain't really all that surprising around here. But one of them being pregnant by a White boy would certainly make heads turn, I'm sure. Speaking of which, here's my White boy now.

"Hey, baby," Jeremy says as he reaches across the passen-

ger's seat, taking my backpack and throwing it into the backseat while I sit down for the short ride up the hill to campus.
If South Bay High didn't have so much drama, it wouldn't be
such a foul place to come to every day. It's a clear morning,
and the unobstructed view to the ocean is always refreshing.

"Hey, Jeremy," I say as we kiss. I haven't spoken to him
since early yesterday afternoon. I stayed up all night with
Mama, working in the spirit room, and didn't get a chance to
call him before that. All I can think about now is Raheem's
lips touching mine. What the hell?

"How was your evening, Lady J?" he says, pulling his Mustang away from the bus stop and joining the rest of the cara-
van rushing to get a good parking space. "I called you, but I
figured you were tired from work." If only he knew the half
of it.

"It was fine. Just hella busy. I had a lot of homework to do
last night," I say, leaving out the spirit-work part of my
evening. I don't think I'll ever be able to share that side of my
life with him, especially since he doesn't believe in God or
anything close to it. If I tell him about my lineage as a
Voodoo Queen, he'll probably react like Misty and think I'm
trying to cast a spell on him. And to think, the first potion I
made was to help keep his ass out of jail.

"I hear you. I'm still making up work from my suspension
weeks ago. The teachers up here are relentless." Yes, they
are, especially when it comes to homework. You'd think we
were in college already.

"*I gotta shake it off. . . .*" Mariah sings, announcing a
phone call. I have to switch up my ring tone every now and
then to suit my mood. The caller ID reveals Rah's name, making me tingle just like I did when he kissed me yesterday.
This isn't good.

"Hey, can you drop me off right here?" I say as we approach the front gate, still in line behind at least twenty other

fancy cars waiting to get into the crowded parking lot. "I need to get something out of my locker before the bell rings," I say, telling only half the truth. I just want some space to think for a little while before the day begins.

"Sure thing, Lady J." God, Jeremy's so sweet, making me feel even guiltier about Rah. When did I become the bad one? "I'll catch up with you at break," he says, leaning over to give me a kiss. His lips are so soft and pleasant. I can't hurt him. I just can't.

As I approach the Main Hall, I see Misty and KJ making out in the quad. They have no shame, although they really should. It still makes my blood boil that they're together, but what can I do? If I really think about it, they deserve each other. Besides, I've got enough dudes to sweat right now.

"I gotta shake it off. . . ." Mariah sings, revealing another call from Raheem. If nothing else, the brotha's persistent.

"What's up, Rah?" I say, sounding irritated, even though I'm glad to hear his voice.

"Well, good morning to you, too, Miss Jackson," he says, sounding as cocky as ever. This boy's confidence is part of what makes him so irresistible. "How's your day going so far, sexy?" he says, making my flushed cheeks obvious, even through the phone.

"It's going just fine, thank you. I'm at school, about to get my day going, so I don't have time to chat, man," I say. Rah, chuckling at my Southern accent, gets to the point of why he's calling.

"I was wondering if you could braid my hair today after school," he says.

"Now, you know Monday's the day I get my assignments for the whole week. I have to organize them and get started on my work for Mama, too. I can't do it tonight," I say. I wish I could though. I love playing in Rah's hair. It's so soft and wavy, black as a panther's coat. And he's wearing it in a fro these days, making him look extra fly.

"You're right. My bad," he says. "Can I come see you anyway?" He sounds like a ten-year-old boy asking his mom's permission go outside and play.

"No, you may not. You're a distraction," I say, sticking to what I know is right but the polar opposite of what I want. I miss having Rah in the spirit room with me. Mama doesn't allow any of my other friends to come in while I'm back there. She makes them wait outside or in the house.

"I'm also good company. I can help you sort the herbs and shit," Rah says, bringing back memories of summer afternoons cleaning Mama's herbs. Rah would help me hang them from the ceiling to dry. He's always been much taller than me. I enjoyed watching his body stretch up toward the ceiling. Yes, he's a huge distraction.

"I'm doing a little more than sorting herbs and shit these days, Rah," I say, sarcastically mimicking him. "I have studying to do, bags to make. It's more complicated than before." When I get to my locker, Nellie and Mickey are there waiting for me. By the looks on both their faces, it's not about to be a drama-free morning.

"Well, holla at your boy when you get a free moment, Miss Jackson," Rah says, momentarily giving up the battle. But I'm sure he's not retreating from the war.

"Fo shizzle," I say, again giving Rah a good laugh before hanging up. Before I can flip my phone, Mickey starts going off about Nellie and her crown.

"You need to check your friend, Jayd," Mickey says, rolling her neck and making her three pairs of descending bamboo earrings jingle. Mickey's quite a sight when she gets pissed. But Nellie's presence has made her look more like a force of nature.

"What the hell happened?" I say, gently pushing Mickey

and Nellie to their opposite sides before opening my locker. The warning bell for first period just rang, and the hall is crawling with students. I need to get all my Spanish books and get to class on time. This mess between the two of them will have to wait until later.

"I'll tell you what happened," Nellie says, straightening her perfectly centered crown on top of her head, making Mickey suck her teeth in disgust. "Your girl here is jealous because everybody's looking at me now and not her ghetto-fabulous ass," Nellie says, putting her hands on her hips and rolling her neck. Although not quite as sassy as Mickey, her chill is still felt, and Mickey's up for the fight.

"You see what I'm talking about, Jayd? This trick is trippin'," Mickey says, looking Nellie straight in the eye. Mickey takes a step toward her, looking like she's about to slap her clear across the face.

"Who you calling a trick?" Nellie says, stepping back from Mickey's approach. Nellie's not a fighter, but she'll be damned if anyone calls her out her name. "You're just a hater, Mickey. You can't stand it when someone else is in the spotlight."

"Okay, you two, calm down. You're causing a scene," I say, placing my books in my backpack before slamming my locker door shut. "Can we discuss this at break? We're all going to be late for class." I lead the way through the busy crowd. It's so loud in here we have to practically shout to hear each other.

"There's nothing to discuss, as far as I'm concerned," Mickey says, sounding like she's done with the chatting.

"I don't have time anyway. I have to prep for my entrance. The Homecoming court is being presented in the Main Quad at lunch, and then we're all going out," Nellie says, flipping her hair over her right shoulder as we exit the hall through the front door into an even busier outside. This girl is getting on my nerves, too.

"Okay, then, we'll talk about it after school," I offer, trying to appease our princess. I hope this phase wears off soon. I'm afraid Mickey's going to whip her ass before it's all said and done.

"I have plans after school," Mickey says. I know she means she's meeting Nigel at football practice. If Nellie found out the two of them were dating, she would flip.

"You know what?" I say, stopping in the middle of the walkway. "You two were friends before I came along. So, y'all work it out. I have enough issues of my own right now to be dealing with this BS." As I head down the path toward Spanish class, I can feel their eyes still on me. Unfortunately for them, they have most of their classes together, including first period. Misty, KJ, C Money, Del and damn near the rest of the Black junior population is on the same track and therefore in the same classes. With the bell ringing above my head, I step into Spanish class and momentarily away from the drama. I'm sure it'll resume soon enough.

Getting through my first two classes smoothly is pivotal for me to have a good morning. And I was able to get some of my homework done in the library during break, giving me more time to work on Mama's assignment, which is also a good thing. But for some reason, this day is determined to be a rocky one. It's lunch, and instead of going off campus with Jeremy and his crew, I'm in the Main Quad waiting for Nellie to appear. Why am I still such a good friend to her?

As Nellie and the rest of South Bay's Homecoming court struts from the cafeteria through the Main Quad, Nigel and our winning football team are escorted by the cheerleaders. Nellie's gleaming and sucking it all in. Tania, right behind her, has a strange look on her face, like she's just smelled something horrible. And then, right on Nellie's back, she throws up.

"Ahhh!" Nellie screams. She's got vomit in her hair, on her neck and back. Tania, embarrassed, runs from the procession back into the cafeteria. Covering her mouth with her left hand, I notice a big diamond ring. This girl's engaged? My dream may be unfolding, but Nellie getting hurled on was an extra perk.

"Damn, that's never going to come out," Reid says into the mic, making light of Nellie's humiliation. I can't stand it. I have to help her. The rest of the court, football team and campus can't contain their laughter any longer.

As I approach Nellie at the front of the quad, I follow her eyes through the crowd, where I see Mickey and Nigel meet up and head toward the front parking lot. Nellie, already hot, has a new fire lit under her now. That was all the validation she needed to know there's something going on between Nigel and Mickey. She looks at me as if I somehow orchestrated this entire event and walks off toward the cafeteria. I should've gone off campus with Jeremy. I've had enough of Nellie's drama for one day.

Thank goodness the day's finally over. Mickey and Nigel never resurfaced after Nellie's unforgettable episode at lunch, so all I have to do is go to my locker and meet up with Jeremy and Chance outside the Main Hall. Damn, I hope I don't run into Misty. That would add to the rest of the day's negativity.

Making my way through the busy hall, I notice my counselor, Mr. Adelezi, talking to some hysterical blond girl. I wonder if he likes his job? Just when I think I'm home free from running into my nemesis, Misty rears her curly head. She must be waiting for her mother to get off. I don't know if Misty's lucky or not, having her mother work in the attendance office. But I'm sure she milks every advantage out of it she can.

As I walk toward her, Misty turns around. Noticing my

gaze, she smiles a twisted grin, licks her lips and blows a kiss at me. That girl works my last nerve. Lucky for her, I'm almost to the front door, where Jeremy and Chance are there waiting for me. Otherwise I might send a kiss of my own back to her.

"Hey, Lady J," Jeremy says, instinctively taking my backpack from my right shoulder and slipping it over his. We hold each other's hands as Chance leads the way. Sprung on Nellie, he starts the conversation off as we exit the front door to chill on the steps for a quick minute before heading home. I sit in between Jeremy's legs, leaning back and ready to give my counsel.

"If you want to get close to Nellie, I suggest you start hangin' out with Tania, Reid and them," I say more than a little salty. After all we've been through, how can Nellie give up our friendship for a crown? It ain't like she's getting paid for it or getting her own reality show.

"Man, those fools are busters. I went to elementary school with them. We used to whip their asses in kick ball. Remember that shit, Jeremy? They've always been little bitches," Chance says, sounding like I really touched a nerve. Jeremy doesn't have to voice his obvious repulsion. He and his brothers have had beef with Reid and his brothers since the beginning of time.

"Well, busters or not, they're Nellie's new crew. Me and Mickey have no influence over anything she does, including who she dates," I say, leaning in close to Jeremy. He bends his arms back, leaning against the cement step, making more room for me.

"That's some stupid shit right there," Jeremy says. "I know Tania's capable of pulling a stunt like that. And Reid's just the punk to help her carry it out. Nellie's jaded if she can't see that—no offense, baby," he says. Like Mama says, everything positive has a negative, names included.

"Yeah, she is acting a bit ignorant these days, and I'm over it. She and Mickey are going at it like two cocks in a fight, and I'm caught in the middle," I say, gently twisting Jeremy's wrist to reveal the time. Our chill time is over, and I need to head home.

"Time up?" he says, knowing the drill. If I still had to take the bus, I'd only be halfway to Compton by now. I'm glad Jeremy enjoys kicking it with me, allowing me a steady ride home.

"Yeah, it's getting late," I say, rising from our cozy spot on the front steps of the office, right across from where the cars are parked. I've lost all feeling in my backside from sitting on the cement steps. But that's all right. At least I got to chill with my baby. I turned my phone off to avoid Rah's after-school harassment. I'm half expecting him to be at my house when I get home.

"All right, y'all. Be safe. And, Jayd, Nellie will come around. I know it," Chance says, with undying faith in her. If I didn't know better I'd say this cat's in love with her.

"You keep on believing that player," I say, following Jeremy to the car. If I know one thing for sure, it's that Nellie's gotten bit by the rich girl's club and would do anything to stay in that clique, including sacrificing her true friends for fake ones.

~ 2 ~
Dangerous Liaisons

*"You might trick me once
No, I won't let you trick me twice."*

—KELIS

Since we now have mandatory AP meetings during break and lunch on Wednesdays, I won't be able to chill at all today. Sometimes this whole AP thing is highly overrated. And when the AP exams come in the spring, I won't have any time to socialize outside of the informal club at all.

I hate these meetings. They're long, boring and led by my least favorite teacher, Mrs. Bennett. After our confrontation about Jeremy, I have no patience for this trick. Her voice and perfume are making me lose my appetite. Usually, I can always eat a Snickers bar—but now it tastes like chocolate-coated perfume. Luckily Mrs. Malone is here to balance the energy.

"Jayd," China says, snapping me out of my little world. I'm glad because I was about to mentally choke Mrs. Bennett in my daydream and get away with it.

"What's up?" I whisper over my shoulder. China's the coolest white girl I've ever known. China's just down and proud to be a white chick from northern California. She kinda reminds me of Mrs. Malone's daughters but even more out there. China's mom committed suicide when she was three, leaving her and her brother to be raised by her dad, a tattoo artist with his bad-ass studio behind their mini mansion. Her house is off the chain, and she has a maid. She can do pretty much whatever she wants.

"Are you going to finish that?" China says, pointing to my Snickers bar. Normally I'd never share this with anyone, but I have little use for it now and I know she's got the munchies. It's only break and this girl's already high.

"No, but it'll cost you," I say, picking the candy bar up from my desk, ready to pass it back.

"How much?" she says. Although I can't see her face, I can tell she's smiling.

"Notes from the meeting at lunch. I can't take any more of this for today," I say.

"I would, but I'm not going to be here either. My man's coming to get me at lunch so we can go surfing. There's going to be a high tide this afternoon," she says, sounding like the surfer chick she is. Must be nice to ditch on a regular basis and not get caught. "But I got you next week, for real," she says, reaching over my shoulder and taking the candy bar, catching Mrs. Bennett's eye.

"I know we agreed to let you eat during the meetings because it's break, but please be ladylike," Mrs. Bennett says, talking to China but looking at me.

"Sorry, Jayd. I got you for break and lunch next week, if you want," China says while devouring the chocolate treat. I'm glad she's enjoying it. It's worth it to me if I can miss an entire day of Mrs. Bennett. The meetings are mandatory, but as long as you can get someone to take notes for you, you won't miss much and the teachers won't trip too hard. They'll just try to make you feel guilty as hell, but I don't care. China takes good notes, and for freedom from Mrs. Bennett, it's worth it.

"All right, China, but don't conveniently come up missing next Wednesday," I say, teasing.

"I got you, Jayd, for real." I'm glad someone does. I feel

less of an attachment to my girls and Jeremy lately, and I don't know what to do about it. For starters, I'm going to talk to Jeremy next period and try to get through to Nellie. I hope they are both open to listening to what I have to say.

Since Tania's vomiting scene on Monday, she and Nellie took yesterday off. But today they're back and feeling as cocky as ever. I guess the whole thing was a personal bonding session between the two of them or something, because they've been inseparable all day. It's already Wednesday, and I have so much schoolwork due on Friday. I already gave up my break again today, and now I have to skip lunch, too. The things a girl will sacrifice for good grades.

As I walk away from my English class toward third period, I see Tania and Jeremy having a heated discussion in the hallway outside our class. I hate that we all have government together. I hate it even more that my dreams are usually right on, which means she's carrying the next Weiner heir. I just wonder if they know it yet. From the looks of it, somebody knows something and I want to know what.

"Hey, Jayd. Where have you been? I've been looking for you everywhere," Mickey says, looking like she's running from the cops. "I need a favor."

"What is it?" She and Nigel have been working my nerves this week, too. Their little affair is causing all kinds of ripples, and I can see a tidal wave coming soon.

"I need you to sign this note for me so my absence from yesterday can be excused," she says like she's asking me to drive the getaway car.

"Hell, no," I say, pushing her letter aside and walking into my classroom. Mickey turns around in hot pursuit.

"Jayd, please! The office won't accept the phone calls from home anymore. They said they needed this signed for Monday's fifth- and six-period absences, but since I wasn't here yesterday, they won't let me back into class until I bring them my note from home. I told them I left it in my locker and I'd bring it at break so they'd let me go to first and second period. Come on, man. Just sign it."

"Why can't you sign it yourself? You've done it a million times," I say, taking my seat before the bell rings. Tania and Jeremy are still outside. I wish I had super hearing. Mickey's distracting me with her drama when I've got business of my own to handle.

"Because I think they're catching on to my handwriting. Look, my homegirl Kitty was making the calls to the attendance office for me, but they said they needed my mother's signature on file for their records. They already had me sign a signature card in my name. You only have to do it this one time. Please." As she begs for me to commit perjury, my teacher, Mrs. Peterson, notices the scene and calls me out, causing the otherwise lively class to come to a screeching halt.

"Miss Jackson, would you mind telling your friend that visiting hours are over?" she says, glaring at me from her desk across the room. That lady gives me the creeps. For the second time today I've been chastised by another teacher I do my best to ignore.

"Mickey, is this all over Nigel? Is it really that serious?" I say, snatching the letter from her hand, scribbling down her mother's name and tossing it back to her.

"Thank you, Jayd. You're my girl," she says, hugging me hard before walking out the door. That girl is too much. But at least I know she won't turn on me, unlike some people. Mickey's a ride-or-die chick for life. And Nellie used to be her road warrior. Now, if she's not careful, Nellie's going to end up dead in Mickey's eyes.

Tania and Jeremy walk into the classroom just as the final bell rings, looking flustered and upset. Now I'm really curious about their conversation. I think my mom should hone her skills for reading people's minds and use it to our advantage. Man, I wish I had her gift.

"Hey, baby," Jeremy says, taking his seat next to mine. He breathes in deeply and then lets out a sigh like he's stressed the hell out. Mrs. Peterson looks at me again like she wants to say something, but she doesn't.

"What's up? You look upset," I say, caressing his left hand with my right. On cue, Tania walks in, giving me and Jeremy a wicked smile.

"I just wish I'd been smarter in the past, that's all," he says, almost letting his conversation with Tania slip. But, like Chris Rock said, even if we know the truth, women always need the confession, and that's exactly what I'm going for.

"Do you want to talk about it? Maybe I can help," I whisper as the final bell rings, signaling the beginning of class. The rest of our conversation will have to wait until after school, but maybe I can still get something out of him indicating he knows about the baby.

"No, it's nothing, really," he says, moving his hand away from mine and picking up his pencil, copying today's agenda from the board. Mrs. Peterson leaves our assignments in the same place on the board every day, and we always start the day off with a quiz. Some of her students say she teaches the same lesson plan every year, right down to her infamous quizzes. "It'll blow over soon, I'm sure."

"Blow over," I say, almost letting my supernatural knowledge slip. How does a baby blow over, I wonder? "Whatever y'all were talking about looked more serious than something that'll just go away." Jeremy stops writing to look me in the eye. It's as though he wants to tell me but can't say the words. I've got to get him to confide in me about this. It's the only way I can help him. I'm sure I can find a way to get the truth out of him, one way or another.

"Oh, and I forgot about our AP meetings after school today and tomorrow. I hate that shit," he says. "I'm sorry, babe. But maybe you can catch a ride with Chance." Truthfully I'm glad for the space. I just wish I had my own ride so I wouldn't have to take three buses to get home. But I'd rather do that today than be forced to talk about my relationship with Jeremy, Nellie or anyone else, and that's exactly what Chance will do. The only person I want to talk to about any of it right now is Mama.

When I get home, Bryan is in the kitchen. He and Jay are excellent cooks, taking after Mama, of course. But neither one of them can hold a candle to me. The hot smell of olive oil popping in the cast-iron skillet makes me hungry, and I'm tempted to ask for a bite. But knowing Bryan, he'll laugh in my face just because he's that greedy.

"What's up, Jayd?" Bryan says, grabbing the oversize container of Lawry's Seasoned Salt and sprinkling it generously over his smothered potatoes and peppers. Damn, his food looks good.

"Same shit, different day," I say, watching him return the container to the kitchen cabinet behind him and grab the metal spatula from the stove, skillfully turning the sizzling potatoes.

"You sound just like Mama, girl. Want to talk about it?" he asks. I know he's genuinely concerned, but I can't trust him with this one. He's friends with Rah, and that's just too close for comfort to discuss me and Jeremy's relationship with him.

"Not with you. You chill with the enemy. But thanks anyway," I say.

"Since when you don't want to talk to your favorite uncle, and what enemy?" he says, testing one of the now golden-brown potatoes with a fork. They smell so good, making my stomach growl like an angry dog. "I know you ain't calling

Rah your enemy," he says, looking satisfied with his culinary skills. "Oh, you must be having issues with that White boy, huh?"

"You know his name, and, yes, it's about him," I say, cutting my eyes. "And who said you were my favorite uncle?" I tease, snatching a potato out of the skillet while heading toward the back door to go check on Mama. I know she has a lot of work to do for her clients, so she's probably in her spirit room.

"You did when you were four years old," he says, scooping most of the potatoes out of the skillet onto his plate. "Here," he says, leaving some for me in the skillet. "Don't say I never gave you nothing."

"Thank you, favorite uncle," I say, taking a fork from the dish rack and slamming the potatoes down.

"By the way, Tarek said hi," he says, leaving the kitchen. Damn, his friend is fine. If I were a few years older, we could work something out, I'm sure. But I have enough boy drama as it is.

After finishing my food, I make my way to the backhouse to join Mama. I'm sure she has plenty of work for me to do.

"Hi, Lexi," I say, stepping over the lounging pooch through the opened door to greet Mama.

"There she is," Mama says, reaching over the full table to kiss me on the cheek without getting up from her stool. "Grab your apron and wash your hands, child. We've got lots of bags to stuff and vials to fill," she says. "These people around here get so scared when Halloween comes around. I ain't gone let them drive me crazy like they did a few years back," she says, pulling up a stool next to hers. There's barely enough room in here for the antique stove and sink, large wooden table and two stools, not to mention the dozens of shelves lining the walls. But everything seems to fit just right.

"Yeah, I remember that," I say, washing my hands in the sink before taking the bright orange apron off the wall next to it. Some of the church folks swear that Halloween is evil and they need something to ward off the impending bad luck it brings every year. Mama always honors the dozens of instantaneous requests for her protection herbs and oils. We work for at least three weeks straight on those things. This year she's getting a jump-start on the crowd.

"Those church people are just so superstitious, and they think I'm some sort of witch who can cast spells," she says, scooping the crushed, dried herbs into her sifter. Mama hates to be compared to a witch. She says that description is more suitable for our neighbor, Esmeralda. "We work with the spirit world and the earth together to influence our reality. All I can do is open the door. They have to attract the protection."

"But, Mama, what we do is a bit magical, isn't it?" I say, picking up the dried herbs from the table and plucking them from their stems. There are about forty more hanging from the ceiling that need to be removed and incorporated into Mama's potions.

"There's nothing magical about inheriting gifts. It's quite natural, if you truly understand the law of attraction and what it means to influence your surroundings. Magic is saying that you have no control, that you need some sort of amulet or wand or something to make shit happen, and that's not the case," she says, giving me an impromptu lesson. "When we make these bags and tonics, Jayd, we are basically influencing people's senses to open their mind's eye to whatever healing or help is needed at the time."

"So, aren't these bags a little magical then?" I say as Mama sifts the herbs into a large wooden bowl, rising from her stool to put them in the large stainless-steel pot of liquid boiling on the stove. It must be at least ninety degrees in here. Luckily it's a mild day—not too hot or cold. So the heat isn't unbearable.

"Only if the client believes they are," she says. "I've had many people return to me demanding their money back because whatever they were asking for didn't come true. That's when I have to counsel them. I don't do repeat potions. If I cast a divination for them and it says their work is incomplete, I tell them that. The work is continual, Jayd. It doesn't end with the bag or baths or dreams. Speaking of which, have you had any lately?" she says, stirring the pot of aromatic herbs.

"No, not since I dreamed about Tania being Jeremy's baby mama the other day," I say.

"Does he know yet?" Mama says, not even questioning that my vision is true. Her confidence in my gifts still scares me sometimes. Most of the time, I wish I were wrong.

"I don't know. I think he does, but he won't tell me. I was actually going to ask you how I could make him confide in me," I say, looking for a little quick magic of my own.

"Trust takes time, Jayd, and there's no potion for that." Damn. I'm still going to look for some magic cupcakes or something when Mama goes to bed.

"But we don't have time," I say, gathering the loose herbs and sifting them into the bowl. My phone, still on vibrate, indicates another text from Rah. That's the third one since I've been home. I'll have to talk to him later. Right now, I've got Jeremy on my mind. "I need to help him now before Tania works her evil on him."

"Concentrate on what you want to happen as a result of this whole mess, Jayd. That's your homework. When you go to school tomorrow, don't engage in the drama at all. Instead, I want you to write down, in the present tense, what you want to happen and how it will affect you," Mama says, turning off the stove and taking her seat at the table, ready for the next round. I have so much homework to do, and it's getting late. I'm going to have to get some of it done at school tomorrow because we could be here all night.

"Can I engage on Friday?" I ask, making light of my task.

"Depends on what you write down tomorrow," Mama says, looking at me in a way that makes me take the assignment more seriously. "It's an exercise that can change your life, Jayd. This is one of the things your mother didn't have the patience to master. Don't make the same mistake," she says.

Tomorrow will be an interesting day of silence for me. Jeremy had to stay after school today and will again tomorrow for his senior AP meetings. Each class meets on a different day and time. So I guess I'll have to wait until Friday to see if my mind can make him trust me enough to confide in me about Tania.

~ 3 ~
War

"Everywhere is war."

—BOB MARLEY

"**A**lways a bridesmaid, never a bride," Mrs. Bennett's *voice says through the loudspeaker. "I told you, you weren't good enough for Jeremy. You should have heeded my warning before, Jayd. You could have saved yourself the embarrassment of getting hurt." What's this trick doing in my dream again?*

"Jayd," a voice calls from the bleachers. We're on the football field at night. But instead of cheerleaders and football players, it's a wedding party, and Jeremy's the groom. What the hell? "Get out of the way! Now!" the voice screams. "You're going to get burned!" The bride, completely veiled, comes down the field in a bright red dress. Stunned by the whole scene, I stand dumbfounded on the field, right in her path.

"Jayd, move!" All of a sudden, the bride speeds up, and a ball of flames ignites behind her. Heading right in Jeremy's direction, she hits me on her path, burning my right arm.

"Ahhh!" I shout, waking up Mama and everyone else in the house.

"Jayd, what's wrong?" Mama says, jumping out of her bed and turning on the lights. I can hear Daddy, Jay and Bryan outside the closed door, ready for a brawl.

"I just had a dream about getting burned," I say, holding my right arm.

"What's going on in there?" Daddy says.

"Nothing. It was just a dream!" I yell through the door. Everyone here is used to my dreams.

"She's okay, y'all. Go back to bed," Mama says, sitting on the bed next to me. I don't know what time it is, but it's early Friday morning and I have to get up for school soon, I'm sure. Mama reaches over my lap, gently twisting my wrist to look at my arm.

"It really hurts," I say, seeing the same thing Mama sees: a big red mark across my arm. Oh, hell, no. Not this shit again.

"When's the last time you had a dream this real?" Mama says, instinctively taking the shea-butter ointment we made last night off the nightstand in between our beds.

"Years ago," I say, remembering a similar dream I had in junior high school. It was around the time my Uncle Donnie passed away. Rah was the only friend I could talk to about it, and he still is.

"Well, there must be a reason why. Your powers are developing quickly, my little fire child." She smiles a wink at me while rubbing the minty salve over my wound. I see nothing amusing about dreaming about fire and getting burned.

I remember the first time it happened. I was about ten years old and staying with my dad for the weekend. I had a dream about getting pushed out of a tree and hitting my head on the cement. My dad questioned me about the huge mark on my forehead the next morning. He didn't believe my story and put me on punishment until I told the truth he wanted to hear. When I got back home to Mama's house and told her what happened, she was so pissed she didn't let me go back over there for almost two months.

"What was the dream about?" Mama says now. The effervescent ointment scent fills the room, calming me down as she begins her usual examination.

"It was about Jeremy marrying a fireball," I say, summing up my dream while sitting straight up in bed. My Tasmanian Devil clock reads five fifteen, which means I have exactly fifteen minutes before my day officially begins. I wish I could go back to sleep, but Mama's ready to give me a quick lesson.

"Are you sure you weren't the fireball?" Mama says, making a joke about one of my many nicknames. "Did anything else happen in the dream?" she says, putting the top back on the jar, listening intently.

"Well, there was a voice warning me, but I didn't recognize it. I couldn't even tell if it was male or female," I say, vaguely remembering the sound.

"It was probably your Ori," Mama says. "Did you read about that in your lessons yet?"

"Uh, no. I didn't know I was supposed to." Like I don't have enough work to do.

"Why would you think you weren't?" Mama says. I can tell she's both irritated and disappointed.

"Because you told me to focus on the whole mind-over-matter thing," I say, impatient with her grilling. My arm's stinging from the ointment. I'm also cranky because my morning hasn't started off right. And having a dream about getting hurt by my boyfriend's future bride from hell is about as bad as it can get.

"Jayd, your lessons are a constant. You must be consistent in your studies no matter if the world around you is falling apart. I shouldn't have to tell you that anymore," she says, giving me chills. "Without them, everything else will be a blur, dreams included," she says, patting me on my hand before returning to her bed. "So tell me about your day of observing yesterday," she says.

"It was actually quite peaceful. Nerve-wracking but peaceful," I say, rising from my small bed, turning off my alarm clock and heading for the door.

"Why nerve-wracking?" Mama yawns.

"Because I wanted so badly to grill Jeremy all day about Tania but didn't. At the end of the day, I didn't feel any worse than when I started out. So it wasn't too bad. But I can't wait to get to school to find out what's really going on."

"Don't be in such a rush, Jayd. That's always been your problem—that and your fiery tongue," she says, pulling up her covers, ready to return to her slumber. Mama needs all the rest she can get. She was up well after midnight working in the spirit room. She had let me go early so I could finish my schoolwork. "The truth will be unveiled in time. And so will your true friends," she says, revealing she knows more about my dream than what I'm telling her.

Why do I even try hiding my dreams from Mama when I know she'll always be in my head, just like my mom? Sometimes I wish I had more control over my powers, mainly my dreams. The last thing I need is for them to physically hurt me. They already stay in my head and affect my social life as it is. I don't need any more interference. I plan on talking to Jeremy after school when he takes me to my mom's. We're supposed to go out for pizza and hang out. I intend on getting to the bottom of what he knows and doesn't know today.

With Mickey and Nigel out for the day and Nellie playing Tania's lapdog, my day was pretty uneventful. Misty and KJ have been hanging so tight it makes my stomach curl to see them together, so I opted to hang with Chance and Jeremy during break and lunch. Now I'm waiting for them both at my locker. The final bell of the day rang ten minutes ago. Where could they be?

Tired of waiting, I decide to walk toward the parking lot.

On my way, I run into Ms. Toni, whom I've been avoiding like the plague these days. There's just too much going on to get grilled by her. Like the other mothers in my life, she'll see straight through my attempt at covering up my true thoughts and get in my head. I can't take any more of that today.

"Hey, Jayd. Now, why haven't I seen you all week?" she says, giving me a big hug. "I've seen more of your little friend Nellie than I have of you lately."

"Yeah," I say, letting go of her tall, slender frame and continuing our walk down the now empty Main Hall toward her office and the front door. "Tell her I said hi," I say, rolling my eyes. That girl has worked my last nerve.

"Why can't you tell her yourself?" Ms. Toni says. It has been a long time since we chatted, and I don't have the time to fill her in on all the drama right now.

"She's too busy hanging with her new crew to spend time with her old one," I say, feeling the sting of my own words. Nellie and I have been tight for the longest, and now the girl won't even return my calls. I'm more hurt than I care to admit. And with Mickey preoccupied running around after Nigel, I'm afraid I won't have my girls anymore.

"Oh, you mean Tania and the rest of the homecoming court," she says, shifting her overstuffed briefcase from her right shoulder to the left before stopping in front of her office door before I enter the Main Hall. "All the hype will be over soon and Nellie will return to her senses, watch and see. She'll get a clear picture of who her real friends are and aren't soon enough, trust me. It happens every year," Ms. Toni says, making light of Nellie's metamorphosis.

"I don't know," I say, leaning up against the wall next to the ASB room where her office is housed. "She's always wanted to be in the rich-kid clique, and now's her chance. I don't think she's going anywhere anytime soon, if she can help it."

"She won't have a choice once she realizes these people aren't really her friends, Jayd. Every year the popular kids pick a few pseudo-popular students to haze. Now, don't get me wrong. Some students new to the clique stick around well after the hazing is over and actually become active members. But others don't, and I'm pretty sure Nellie's a member of the latter. She's going to need her real friends when this whole homecoming thing is over. I hope you know that," Ms. Toni says, making me feel a little bad for Nellie.

"Well, I don't know about Mickey. She's too busy making an enemy out of Nellie on her own accord. I'll try to be here for her, but she's making it very difficult."

"That's what real friends do, girl. You young people and your impatient ways," she says, standing in the open door, removing the heavy bag from her shoulder and placing it on the ground. "All relationships take work, time and consistency. You have to be there during the good times and the bad, when they show both their beautiful smiles and their ugly behinds. You have to take the good with the bad and, above all, be patient." Damn, she sounds just like Mama. And I know they're both right.

"Hey, babe," Chance says, picking me up from behind, catching me and Ms. Toni off guard.

"Boy, put me down," I say, slapping his hands from around my waist as he returns my feet to the ground.

"Hi, Ms. Toni," Chance says, giving her a hug, too. You can't help but love his spirit.

"Hi, Chance. Bye, Jayd," Ms. Toni says, picking up her bag and heading toward her office. "And, Jayd, remember what I said. I want to see you next week, you hear me?" She gives me a hug before allowing the door to close behind her.

"What the hell took you so long? And where's Jeremy," I say, realizing it's been twenty-five minutes since the bell rang.

"He had some unexpected business to take care of, so he

told me to come and swoop you up and meet him at the pizza spot. You cool," he says, noticing my disappointment. I haven't spent much quality time with Jeremy this week, and I know this business has to do with Tania. I wonder how much Chance knows.

"So what business did he need to take care of? He's not selling weed again, is he?" I say, knowing Jeremy's days of slanging are over. Still, I've got to start the grill off as slow and innocent as possible if I want the full confession.

"Come on, girl. I'm starving for a Hawaiian slice right now. You got all your stuff?" he says, taking my backpack from my shoulder and my GAP bag from my hand before leading me into the main office, toward the front where his Classic Nova's parked.

"You didn't answer my question. What business did Jeremy have that was so important he left his girlfriend waiting?" He opens the passenger door, allowing me to slide into the warm leather seats before he passes me my backpack. I place both my weekend bag and backpack on the floor. I love this car.

"Look, I don't know nothing," he says, taking his seat and starting the engine. The loud music blares out of the speakers, but I'm used to it. One of the rules in Chance's car is that you must deal with the bass. "I'm just doing a favor for the homie, know what I'm saying?" Chance says, being a loyal friend. But he's my friend too, and if there's something I need to know about Jeremy, he should tell me.

"Does it have anything to do with Tania?" I say. Judging from the tension in his jawbone, I'm dead on. "What the hell is really going on, Chance? Don't you think I deserve to know?" I attempt to make him feel guilty.

"Look, this is out of my territory. It gets too messy when friends date sometimes. And I'm removing myself from the middle of this one," he says, pulling the car away from the school toward Pacific Coast Highway. It's foggy and a bit cool outside, which is good for me. With the burn mark from last night's dream on my right arm, I wanted to cover up today. So I opted for my lavendar Lerner jogging suit with a white tank underneath the jacket. Comfy, cute and warm.

"You can't do that. You're smack dab in the middle of this one, so get to talking," I say like the sassy Black girl he knows and loves. "I think you forget who you're talking to sometimes. You think I'm just your homeboy's girl, but I was your friend first."

"Word has it you been doing a little moonlighting of your own," he says, making me blush. Just then a call comes in from Rah. "That's your boy now, huh?" Damn, how'd he know?

"Ain't nobody moonlighting," I say, defensive. "You know Rah and I are just friends."

"I know that, and maybe you know that. But does Rah know that?" Chance says, pulling up to Pizza by the Slice.

"Yes, he knows that," I say, lying through my teeth. "And you know what? All of that is irrelevant. I asked you about Jeremy and Tania, so give it up." I open my door and step out. The smell of the pizza makes me instantly hungry. I never made up for the Snickers I missed earlier this week at lunch, so I'm going to tear my slice up. I notice Jeremy's Mustang parked on the other side of the cramped lot, next to Tania's BMW. No, this trick isn't here with my man.

"Oh, it's on," I say, slamming the car door shut and marching toward the front door. I've had enough of being kept in the dark, especially when I already know the truth. Ever since he told me he loved me last weekend, we haven't had any time to ourselves for very long. I've been looking forward to us kicking it all day, and now this heffa's messing up my moment. Following my gaze across the parking lot,

Chance notices the Roadster and grabs my arm, not knowing he's causing me pain.

"Let go of me," I say, snatching my now throbbing arm out of his hand and marching toward the restaurant. Chance's phone rings, causing him to stay behind while I march in, ready to attack.

The hot, aroma-filled air hits me like a wave but not hard enough to distract me from my mission: finding Jeremy. As I walk toward the cozy booths lining the place, I see Tania and her crew, Nellie included.

"Hey, Jayd," Tania says. Nellie looks up from her bottled water and gives me a fake smile. She looks like she's lost about ten pounds in the past week. She didn't eat much before, and I bet since hangin' out with these girls, it's even less now.

"What's up, Nellie?" I say, ignoring Tania completely. I know it's no coincidence she's here at the same time as Jeremy, no matter how it may appear. "Have you checked your messages lately?"

"I've just been really busy. You know, homecoming stuff," she says, sounding like the bitch she's become.

"Homecoming's over, Nellie," I say, tired of her mantra. "Tell her, Tania. Y'all do this every year," I say, repeating what Ms. Toni told me earlier. Someone has to open Nellie's eyes before she really gets hurt. "You take on a couple of clueless wannabes and haze them until you get bored. Isn't that right, Laura?" I say, redirecting my venom at Reid's girlfriend. They've been setting up Nellie from jump, and I'm going to prove it.

"You're just a hater," Laura says in her worst Black-girl imitation ever. "Why don't you get over yourself and go back to the CPT or whatever you guys call it." She tosses her long brown hair over her slightly freckled shoulders. Oh, no, this bitch didn't just dis my hometown. I want to slap the shit out of her, but she's not my immediate concern—Nellie's dim-witted ass is.

"Nellie, what the hell is wrong with you?" I yell, now causing a scene. I see Jeremy coming from the bathroom headed our way. I better wrap this up so I can get back to my main priority—he and Tania. "This trick just insulted our home, and you still sitting here? They're playing you, girl. Can't you see that?"

"You're embarrassing me," Nellie says between her teeth. She looks mortified, like I just walked in the spot with my house shoes on and rollers in my hair, in my bathrobe, spitting sunflower seeds on the floor.

"Embarrassing you? Have you looked in the mirror lately? You look like Whitney after Bobby, and I'm sick of your attitude," I say as Jeremy walks up to the booth. Chance is still on the phone outside, totally unaware of the scene I've just caused. But these heffas are stringing my best friend along, and I just can't stand by and watch. Not when Tania's the one doing it. This is war, and I'm ready for battle.

"Hey, baby," Jeremy says, putting his arm around my waist and kissing my cheek. "What's all the commotion about?"

"I'm trying to convince my girl here that Tania's a scheming bitch who's only out to hurt her," I say, staring Nellie down and ignoring Tania's reaction. Where's Mickey when we need her? She lives for fronting chicks. "By the way," I say, redirecting my gaze at the ringleader, "I know you're after my man."

"Oh, sweetie," I've already had him, remember?" she says, taking a bread stick from the basket on the table and biting the tip. I lunge at her, snatching it out of her mouth and throwing it in her face.

"You're a twisted broad, aren't you, Tania?" I say as Jeremy holds me back and Chance runs in to see what all the fuss is about.

"What the hell happened in here?" Chance says.

"I'm going to file a complaint against your little ghetto ass!" Tania yells. "First my Blackberry, now this? Anger management might do you some good."

"Shut the hell up talking to me, Tania," I say as Jeremy leads me away from the booth toward the front door. I guess our pizza date is ruined. "Nellie, don't trust them. They're not your real friends!"

"Can you believe that trick?" I say, breaking free of Jeremy's tight grip as we walk toward Chance's car.

"What happened?" Chance says, jogging the short distance to his car and grabbing my bags. He knows Jeremy's pissed, and Chance wants to get away from the crime scene now. He really doesn't have to leave. But I guess he wants to eat in peace. And seeing Nellie with those heffas can't be peaceful for him. He really has it bad for my girl and hates to see her with them, even if he doesn't react like me. I feel like I'm doing both our jobs.

"For what it's worth," Chance says, walking us to Jeremy's car, "I'm with you, Jayd. Those broads aren't good for my Nellie." He leans up against the Mustang and lights a cigarette. I hate the smell of those things. At least he's on the driver's side, next to the witch's broomstick. I wish I could make my mind key Tania's car. Lucky for her my powers don't work like that.

"What's wrong with you?" Jeremy says, opening the car door and forcing me inside. "Why can't you control your temper?" He grabs my bags from a very amused Chance.

"We'll find a way to save Nellie, don't worry," Chance says, coming around to my side and giving me a hug. "Don't ever change, girl. And I hope Nellie realizes what a good friend she has in you." Chance is one of my first friends at South Bay, and I love him like a brother.

"Thanks, man, and we'll talk later," Jeremy says, opening the driver's-side door and getting in.

"No prob. And you knew you had a fiery one. That's why you like her, so don't trip too hard, bro," Chance says, heading back across the small lot toward his car, defending me like a good big brother does. Judging Jeremy's facial expressions, it doesn't look like Chance's words had much of an impact on him. He looks hotter than I feel. But I'm still hungry.

"Since you made me leave, can we at least stop and get something else to eat?" I pout. I'm in no mood to argue with Jeremy now. And I still want to get the truth out of him about his run-in with Tania the other day, so I've got to calm his ass down, and that starts by me chilling out, which can't happen if I'm hungry.

"Not until you tell me what the hell that was all about back there," he says, speeding down Pacific Coast Highway toward Inglewood. "What is it with you and being loud?"

"Now you're just being mean," I say. "You can't keep me from eating. You ain't my daddy."

"I know that. But, Jayd, for real: every time you feel like mouthing off at someone, you can't," he says, pulling up to Fatburgers. Aw, hell, yeah. A turkey cheeseburger will definitely hit the spot.

"Why not?" I say, practically jumping out of the car. "If someone's disrespectful, they must be checked." As we enter the packed restaurant, the loud seventies music booming out of the jukebox on the wall keeps us from finishing our conversation. Jeremy places our orders, and I find a seat outside. The moist fog actually feels good on my warm skin. I'm still flustered from our run-in and need to cool off.

"Here's your strawberry shake," Jeremy says, handing me the oversize indulgence. "Now what are we going to do about this temper of yours?" He sounds less angry but still annoyed. "It's not good for you, nor is it always called for. You can't let Tania get a rise out of you. That's what she lives for. You've got to know how to play her. Otherwise she wins." He sips his root beer and takes a seat.

"I don't give a damn about her rules. I just want her out of my life," I say, sucking my thick shake through the fat straw. A chill goes down my spine, causing me to sit up straight and take note of the thought I just put into motion. That I wish Tania gone aren't just empty words. I mean them. I want her gone, just like that trick Trecee who caused all that drama with KJ. And according to my dream about Tania moving to New York, she should be on her way out.

"She will be, soon enough," Jeremy says, almost telling me what he knows. He looks sullen, like someone just stole his bike. So he does know about the baby. But I still want him to tell me the truth.

"What do you mean by that?" I ask, readjusting myself in the hard, wire chair. Between the shake and the cool air, I'm starting to get uncomfortable.

"Nothing. Are you cold?" Jeremy asks, instinctively removing his poncho and momentarily revealing his tight stomach and chest before his Nike T-shirt falls back down over the top of his jeans. "Here."

"Thank you," I say, placing it over my head. It's so warm and smells like Irish Spring, just like him. "What did you mean about Tania being gone soon? Where's she going?" I hope he says New York.

"I just mean she'll have no time to be bothered with all this nonsense soon," he says, expertly evading my question. "I'll check to see if our food's ready." He leaves me alone to my thoughts. This dude is too good, but I know he knows. I'll have to redirect my efforts in another direction to get me some inside info. But how? Maybe after some good food I'll come up with some better ideas. For now, I'm going to enjoy my juicy burger, fries and my man.

~ 4 ~
The Other Side

"Here is something you can't understand/
How I can just kill a man."

—CYPRESS HILL

Before dropping me off at my mom's last night, Jeremy and I had an impromptu make-out session at the beach. Needless to say, we didn't get much talking done. And with me working all day and him night-surfing with his brothers tonight, we won't get to chat too much today either. Rah wants me to come through this evening's session. I know I probably shouldn't, especially since the last time I saw him, he had me in a lip-lock. But I'm definitely going to think about it.

"Excuse me, miss. Is this seat taken?" this nice-looking elder sister says to me. The bus is packed for a Saturday morning. I wish my mom would wake up early and take me to work, but I know that's asking for a bit much. She has to get up early Monday through Friday, so the weekends are her days to sleep in.

"No, it's not," I say, readjusting myself in the small double seat, making extra room for her. My stop's coming up soon. Thank goodness Simply Wholesome isn't far from Inglewood. I don't want to be on this cramped bus any longer than necessary.

"I gotta shake it off," Mariah sings, announcing a phone

call from Rah. What's he doing up at seven in the morning? Usually he'd just be wrapping up a session right about now.

"What's up?" I say, instantly annoying the lady sitting next to me. She gives me a look as if to say she's disgusted with my entire generation for talking on our cells in public. Well, at least I'm not like the loud dudes at the back of the bus, cussing like sailors and not caring who hears. Mama taught me better than that. But talking on my cell's a whole other thing.

"Nothing. Just calling to see what you're doing today," he says. Damn, he sounds good in the morning.

"I'm on my way to work," I say. I reach up and grab the alarm string, signaling the driver to stop at La Brea and Over-hill, right in front of my job. I have a few minutes to spare be-fore clocking in, so I can catch up with him for a sec.

"Why haven't you returned my calls from yesterday? White boy keeping you busy?" he says, sounding jealous. I have to admit, I love keeping Rah on his toes with Jeremy. Being a re-cent victim of game playing, I should know better, but I'm sure Rah understands what he's getting himself into with me.

"You've got some nerve trying to grill me," I say, exiting the bus. I glance back through the window, watching the old lady stretch across both sides of the seat, relieved to have the space all to herself. I know just how she feels. "How's Trish?" I say, doing a little grilling of my own.

"She's fine," Rah says. "But not as fine as you." Rah thinks his game is tight, but he knows the shit don't work on me.

"Whatever, Rah. Why are you calling me so early? Shouldn't you just be falling asleep?" I say, taking a seat on the bench outside the front door. I can see Alonzo and Sarah chilling in his car before we start our day. I nod a quick "what's up" at the two of them. The time always goes by faster with my two favorite coworkers working the same shift as me.

"I just wanted to get your day started off with me on your

mind." I didn't need him to call for that to happen. He's on my mind more often than not lately. Even while I was chilling last night with Jeremy, I kept thinking how Rah would have handled the situation with Tania. He would have had my back one hundred and ten percent. And Rah loves my fiery side, unlike Jeremy. I think he was about as embarrassed as Nellie looked yesterday, and if that's the case, we have a bigger problem than Tania's spawn.

"Well, thank you for the shout-out. It's much appreciated." Shahid's immaculate black Jaguar pulls up in front of the restaurant, with Summer not far behind. I'm so glad our new shift manager, Marty, isn't here yet. She irks the hell out of us all. But apparently she is the best person for the job—businesswise—or at least that's what the employees were told.

"Will we see you tonight at the session?" Rah says. I can hear his little brother Kamal in the background asking for me. It's hard to turn both of them down, but I've had all the drama I can handle for the week. I need some peace.

"It depends," I say, giving him a hard time. "Who's this 'we' you're talking about?"

"Me, Kamal, Nigel and your girl," Rah says, referring to Mickey. "We get good shit done when y'all are around. For real, y'all got good vibes, especially you, Jayd. You gotta come through. It's the only time I get to kick it with you now, unless it's some sort of function coming up you need an escort for." I'm going to do my best to keep him from coming to the Masquerade Ball. Although if Nigel's going to be there, I'm sure Rah already has a costume picked out. I know Jeremy won't be going, after all we went through with him not accompanying me to homecoming. And that's where Rah made his best moves, other than the kiss last weekend.

"I really have a lot of spirit work I need to catch up on, not to mention my English portfolio's due at our next meeting,"

I say. And I'm telling the truth. Although I don't plan on being at the meeting, I do plan on turning in my completed notebook to Mrs. Malone in class that morning. I'll just tell her I have another club meeting or a counseling session or something. She'll let me slide as long as the portfolio's in good order.

"Oh. Well, you know a nigga don't want to intrude on your work and all. But if you could fit me in your schedule, holla at your boy," Rah says, making me giggle. He can be so silly sometimes.

"I will. Now let me get to work," I say, actually beginning to dread the long day. If I didn't have to deal with customers, it would be all right. But these bougie-ass people around here work the hell out of my nerves sometimes. A few of them are cool, though.

"All right, shawty. Get at me if you want a ride home," he says. Now, I might just take him up on his offer.

"I'll do that," I say before hanging up and following Shahid and Summer in.

"Good morning, Jayd," they say simultaneously. For two people who aren't a couple, they sure do behave like one.

"Good morning," I say as Sarah and Alonzo join us, ready to start the day. Supreme, the opener for the store, is already in the back taking inventory. We're ready to get it cracking. I'm going to call Jeremy at lunch just to see what's up with him. It sucks that we won't have time to kick it today. I really do miss our extended coffeeshop talks or just hanging out with him. I'll just have to wait until tomorrow to see him. He's supposed to pick me up from my mom's and take me to his house for dinner, but we'll see. It'll be the first time he takes me all the way home to Mama's house.

After this morning's surprise call from Rah, I've been wondering if I should just go on and go to the session tonight. I can probably get a ride from Nigel or Mickey, if I really want to. But right now I want to talk to my man while I still have some time left on my lunch. Before I can dial, the phone rings, signaling a call from my dad. Here we go.

"Hey, Daddy," I say in a voice that lets him know I'm glad he's alive and now we can hang up.

"Hey, Jayd," he says, sounding almost the same. At least the feeling's mutual. I know I'm his least favorite kid because I'm different in his eyes. And he hates the fact that I show more loyalty to my mother's folks than his. But what else am I supposed to do? I've lived with them all my life because my parents can't get it together, and he's the main reason why. I'm sure we could use some sort of counseling or something, but it's not just anger. We'd need a whole exorcism to get rid of these family demons.

"What's up, Daddy? I'm just clocking in to work," I say, literally taking my time card and punching it in. I put my wannabe-Coach bag under the register and grab my apron from the wall before washing my hands in the sink.

"Yeah, I forgot today was a workday for you. Listen, did you still want to take driving lessons?" he says, like we just had this conversation yesterday. I asked him if he would pay for those lessons when I turned sixteen in March, and that was months ago. What the hell?

"Uh, yeah. That was what I wanted for my sixteenth birthday present," I remind him. "I thought you forgot."

"Nah, I didn't forget. And you need to mind your sass, little girl," he says, making me roll my eyes. I can't wait until I don't need money from my parents anymore. I wish I could start my own business now and just support myself. I'd move out of Mama's, get my own spot and just work and go to school. That would be heaven. But who am I kidding? Mama will never let me move now. "Well, I set it up for the next month through the company I used to work for. So give them a call and give them your schedule," he says, taking me off guard. That's my daddy though. And, also like him, I'm sure there's a price to be paid.

"Why now? What's the catch?" I say, suspicious of his good deeds, as usual. Mama taught me well.

"Well, I just want you to get your license, that's all. Then maybe we could see a little more of you over here." I knew it. He wants to be able to tell his family he's a great dad and that I owe him my driving freedom because he paid for it. I know it. But, whatever. If it'll get me off the bus and keep me from being dependant on others for my ride, then so be it.

"Cool. Thanks," I say, trying to sound appreciative. "If you could just leave the info on my voice mail, I'll call when I get off."

"Why can't you write it down now?" he says, conveniently forgetting I'm at work, even if I am on my lunch.

"Because I don't have a pen right now," I say, telling the truth. And, this barbecue veggie burger is too messy and damned good for me to stop eating and write anything.

"Okay, Jayd. But you're getting too spoiled," he says before hanging up. I wish that were the case. If my dad only knew all the shit I do on a daily basis. And then I work all weekend, too. If this is spoiled, then I'd rather be ripe. I think I'll call Rah for that ride after all.

"Jayd, you plan on working today?" Marty says, ruining my whole vibe. Why does she have to sweat me so hard? They're aren't even any customers right now, and I still have five minutes left before clocking back in.

"Yes, when it's my time to work," I say, returning to making my quick phone call to Rah.

"Jayd," she says, leaning up against the unstable metal table, making my smoothie tilt slightly, dripping on its side. "You're going to have to learn to work as a team if you want to grow here." Is this trick serious? Like it's my life's aspiration to be a cashier—please. Both Summer and Shahid want us all to rise above the norm.

"Look, maybe this is the job you prayed for when you were a little girl," I say, picking up the napkin next to my cup and wiping up her mess. "But not me. Now, if you'll excuse me, I still have four more minutes left, and I have another call to make." I push Rah's name on my phone, ignoring Marty completely. She has no choice but to leave me alone now, or so I think.

"We're going to have to talk more about your attitude, Jayd," she says, finally walking away and giving me some privacy. Damn, she makes my butt itch.

"Jayd, what's cracking?" Rah says, sounding like I woke him from a good nap.

"I'm sorry. I was just taking you up on your offer, but if you're asleep, it's all good," I say, feeling bad for calling. I know he's a nocturnal being.

"Nah, girl. I just dozed off for a sec," he says. "Yeah, I got you, girl. Call me right before you get off and I'll be there."

"Thanks, boo. Now get back to sleep," I say. I'm so thankful Rah's back in my life, even if we can be only friends. The thing about staying friends is that there's no danger in crossing over to the other side of love: hate. I never felt both emotions so strong until I met Rah. Besides, they say the grass is always greener, or in this case, the water's bluer on the other side. But I don't know. If Rah didn't have a girlfriend and I wasn't with Jeremy, who knows where we'd be.

"Yeah, I'll see you later, shawty. Peace," he says, hanging up the phone. Now I have to get back to work. I can't wait until my shift is over in a few hours so I can see Rah. It feels like it's been forever. I hope he's doesn't try to kiss me again. I'll try to resist, but I can't make any promises.

As I walk back into the restaurant, the line is very long, and Sarah looks like she's about to snap. That's Simply

Wholesome. It's never without customers for long, and that's also what makes the day go by fast. Hopefully it'll stay busy until I get off at five. That way, Marty won't have a chance to get on me for stupid crap, and I won't have a chance to think about Rah kissing me again.

It's a quarter to five, and I already sent Rah a text saying it's time to wake up and get here soon. The rest of the day flew by, thank God. And now I'm ready to shower and chill for a while.

"Jayd, can I speak to you for a minute?" Summer says. Shahid's already gone for the day, and Summer's on her way out with me. Alonzo and Sarah got off an hour ago.

"Sure, Summer. Let me just grab my purse," I say, removing my apron and hanging it back on the hook next to the time clock before following her into the small office between the restaurant and the store. I take a seat in the chair next to hers across from the desk.

"Jayd, Marty says you have a problem with insubordination," Summer begins. "And being that she's your supervisor, you're going to have to start showing her a little respect."

"Summer, I've been working here for over a year. Have I ever caused any problems?" I say, feeling my temperature rise. If it's one thing I can't stand, it's a trick starting some mess that could affect my money. I can't afford those kinds of games.

"No, Jayd, and we love you," she says, speaking for both herself and Shahid. "But Marty's going to be taking over the weekend shifts for us. We'll still open, but she'll come in at lunch and finish the day. So you're going to have to find a way to get along with her," she says, giving me a hug. "Just make it easy for yourself, girl. You don't have to fight every battle." As she releases my vexed frame, my phone vibrates. It's Rah saying he's here.

"Can I go now?" I say. I'm not really mad at her, just fed up for the day.

"Sure sweetie," Summer says, rising to leave the office with me. "See you in the morning." Don't remind me. I'm starting to hate this gig.

As I walk outside, the warm evening air caresses my cheeks like a soft shawl. It feels good to be off and to have a ride home. My feet are barking, and I could use some loud music with lots of bass to get my troubles off my mind. The red Acura Legend's speakers are blaring Alicia Keys and Cham's "Ghetto Story," calling me to be healed. Reggae always does the trick for me. I might have to make this my new ring tone. Or just use it as a personal one for Rah.

"What's up, Jayd?" Kamal says, jumping out of the passenger's seat to get in the back.

"Hey, boo," I say, giving Kamal a bear hug before he squeezes into the backseat. I flip the passenger's seat back up.

"How was work?" Rah says, securing my chair before I sit down; I fully absorb the new-car-scented tree and listen to the music. I feel on top of the world right now.

"Work," I say, not wanting to bring myself down. "How was sleep?" I cut my eyes at him. He looks so good in his red Phat Farm polo shirt and jeans with his silver chain blinging against his chocolate skin. If it weren't for his Muslim upbringing, he would probably be sporting platinum and diamonds like everyone else. But Rah's father raised him to be more humble than that.

"Sleep," he says. "I wanted to know, if you had time, could you hook a brotha up with some braids?" He rubs his hands through his untamed Afro. "I told them we're starting the session at eight. So that gives us a few hours to chill before."

"Yeah, but it's going to cost you," I say, locking my fingers in his thick hair and gently rubbing his head.

"What?" Rah says, turning down the volume slightly to hear my price. He looks like he's enjoying the impromptu massage. Mama likes the way I rub her hair when I braid it, too. She taught me that trick. It stimulates the scalp and relaxes the client before you start pulling the braids into place.

"Y'all will have to wait while I change. I've been working all day, and I need a quick shower," I say as we pull away from my job, heading toward Inglewood. The sun's beginning to set, and all the freshly washed cars on the streets are starting to glisten.

"No problem, Queen Jayd," Rah says, giving me a sly wink. "What happened to your arm?" The burn's physical mark is almost gone. But the psychological pain is still with me.

"I had a dream," I say, removing my hand from his head and staring out my window, allowing the bass to massage my forehead.

"Oh," Rah says, not pushing me further. There's no need to; he already has a vivid idea of what I'm going through. He's always been so patient and understanding, almost making me forget how much he hurt me back in the day. But he's always been a good friend.

After a quick shower and change, Rah takes us back to his house for our braid session before the real one begins. I miss braiding his soft hair. It shines like granite with the coconut oil Mama and I made some time ago. I love the way it smells, and it's the perfect texture for braiding. I use it for my cornrows all the time.

"I miss being in between your legs," he says, being a little too descriptive for me.

"Shut up, fool. Why you gotta be nasty about it?" I say, smacking Rah in the head and making him laugh. But he can feel I miss braiding his hair, too.

"Rah, Trish is here," Kamal says. Before Rah can get up,

Trish is through the door with Nigel's girlfriend, Tasha, right behind her. I saw a picture of all them together in last year's yearbook.

"What's up, Jayd?" Trish says, sounding hella faded. She smells like she's been drinking all day, and she's got a blunt in her hand. This can't be good. It's almost eight, and Mickey and Nigel should be rolling up soon, adding more shit to the mix. I need to call and warn Mickey.

"What the hell are you doing here?" Rah says, answering for me. "I told you I was busy tonight, Trish." He doesn't move from his cozy spot on the floor, his now completely cornrowed head between my thighs. I know these bourgie-ass girls don't know how to braid.

"I came to see what was so important you couldn't pick me up from my nail appointment. And now I know," Trish says, flinging her long, curly black hair over her shoulder and giving me hella attitude. Why are there heffas everywhere I go?

"Jayd's braiding my hair before the session. So what?" Rah says. One thing about Rah is that he never breaks his cool. Getting caught ain't no big deal to him, because he rarely gets caught in a full lie. He's a professional at evading the truth without incriminating himself. Speaking of criminal activity, I need to warn Mickey before she and Nigel walk in, setting Trish and Tasha completely off.

"What's the big deal?" Trish says, raising her drunken voice, making Kamal run for cover. I guess he's used to her going off. She actually reminds me a lot of Rah's mom, who's rarely here. "The big deal is this bitch is your ex-girlfriend, and I'm tired of seeing her ghetto ass over here, that's what." Oh, no, this bitch didn't just call me a bitch.

"Why you gotta go there, Trish? Jayd, I'll be right back. Don't go anywhere," he says, pointing toward the back door and marching Trish out of the studio with Tasha right behind her before I have a chance to go off. It's probably for the best. How can I get out of here now? Let me call Mickey. But before I can dial her number, the commotion outside gets louder. I have to see what's going on.

"What are y'all doing here together?" Tasha says to a stunned Nigel and Mickey, who are walking up the front porch as we are all headed out. Aw, hell, no. It's about to be on, and I still have oil on my hands. I can't get my earrings off like this. I need to think fast. I don't feel like being in a fight with these tipsy broads right now. It wouldn't be fair. And if I ever do whip Trish's ass, I want her to know it was an even win.

"Mickey, girl, thank you for picking me up," I say, even though Mickey looks like she's ready to throw down. Nigel's got my girl sprung. I know her man's getting suspicious. "They need to get started on the session. You're just in time," I say, passing up Rah, Trish and Tasha to grab Mickey's arm and head back down the driveway. "Rah, I'll get my twenty dollars next time. Peace, Nigel," I say, leading us toward the car. Everyone's shell-shocked at how I'm handling the tense situation. But I just don't have time for all this. I'd rather be at home getting some work done if the session's not going to be productive. And Mickey's the one who'll have to get me there.

"Jayd, what are you doing?" Mickey whispers, walking quickly beside me toward the pink Regal parked next to the curb. "We can take those skanks."

"That's not the point," I say, opening the passenger's door and getting in. "This isn't our battle." I look over my shoulder at the scene through her tinted windows. Everyone's going back inside except for Rah, who turns around and catches my eye. As we pull off, he mouths "call me" and looks regretful as he turns around to go back inside and deal with his drama.

"What the hell are you talking about?" Mickey says, instinctively turning her car toward Compton. Noticing her arm glistening, she takes a napkin out of her armrest to wipe it off. "And what's that on your hands?"

"Coconut oil. I'm sorry I got it on your arm, but you can rub it in like lotion. It won't hurt you," I say, laughing at her silly self.

"I already have some on, and it's making my skin tingle," she says, now looking for another napkin in her pink fur-covered glove compartment. Her man had her classic Regal hooked up earlier this year for her sixteenth birthday. "I won't ask what you and Rah were using it for," she says, taking the crumpled napkins and frantically wiping her skin.

"Shut up. I have a man and a date tomorrow. I'm not trying to get too caught up with Rah, unlike you and Nigel, who don't seem to care that you each have significant others."

"Well, I think you need to think more about that plan," Mickey says, completely ignoring my moral warning. "Rah seems to really dig you, Jayd. And he's much finer than Jeremy."

"Girl, can you please just take me back to my mom's and stop trying to lure me over to the dark side?" Where's Nellie's uptight ass when I need her? "I need to study," I say, choosing to ignore the phone calls and text messages coming in from Rah. Mickey's phone is ringing, too. I guess the chicken heads have now left the building and it's safe to return. But this little queen's done for the night. I want info from Jeremy, and I need rest to be as sweet as it's going to require for me to get it.

"What? You don't want to go back?" she says, immediately turning the car back around.

"No. I have a lot of work to do, and I'm tired from working all day. Besides, what's to stop Tasha and Trish from coming back? I'm not in the mood for all this mess tonight,

Mickey. Please take me back to Inglewood," I say, sending Rah a similar message. I just want to go home, study my lessons and maybe eat some chocolate Nutter Butters, if my mom left me any in the refrigerator. I just want to chill and focus on making Jeremy tell me the whole truth and nothing but the truth tomorrow. Everything else will have to wait.

~ 5 ~
Revelations

"Though my eyes saw the deception/
My heart wouldn't let me learn."

—FUGEES

I don't like walking home in my mom's neighborhood. I feel more exposed with all the apartments around here. I told Jeremy he could pick me up from here an hour after I got off work, which was thirty minutes ago. I need to change out of my work clothes, and I didn't want him to wait with my mom. She's liable to grill him again, and I don't need him tense, not today. Besides, I don't think he's all that comfortable over here, unlike Rah. Too bad my mom wasn't home when he and Kamal came by yesterday. I'm sure they have some catching up to do.

Approaching the long driveway leading toward my mom's apartment, I see her gray Mazda parked in its stall. I wonder if she'll let me drive it when I get my license. I forgot to tell her about my dad paying for my driving lessons. I know she'll have something to say about that. Maybe I should save that information for next weekend.

"Hey, baby. How was your day?" my mom says, sprawled across the cozy couch. She knows Jeremy's picking me up today so she's decided to lounge until she goes to work tomorrow morning, I guess. Ever since things went sour with Ras Joe, she's been chilling at the house more. Yesterday she was out with her homegirl Vivica for a girl's day. But, unlike my mom, Vivica's married and has children at home, leaving her little time to play.

"It was okay," I say, closing the door behind me before heading straight for the bathroom. I've had to pee since I clocked out, but I didn't want to give Marty the opportunity to say anything else to me. It was hard enough following Summer's advice of making it easy for myself by being unresponsive to Marty's stupid comments, but I've been at my wit's end all day. It can't be good for me or my bladder to hold my tongue like that. But until I figure out another way to make some cash flow, I'll have to take all the shit she shovels my way.

"Jayd, what time is Jeremy picking you up?" my mom yells from the couch. We can practically hear each other breathe, the walls are so thin in this apartment.

"In about half an hour," I say, washing my hands and quickly undressing. As I open the door and head for her room where my weekend bag is, I can hear my mom pouring herself a drink in the kitchen. I'd bet money it's Bailey's Irish Cream. I quickly change into some Old Navy jeans and an orange GAP shirt. We're supposed to hang out by the pier and have coffee, so low key is definitely the way to go.

"How are your studies going?" my mom says, noticing me put my spirit notebook into my backpack beside the couch before finding my sandals and slipping them on. If I could, I'd wear them every day of the year. "Has Mama given you any new assignments?" she says, reclaiming her position on the couch and forcing me to sit in a chair at the dining table across the room.

"Well, sort of." I recall the writing exercise she gave me last week. "Mama told me to focus on what I want most and write it down in the present tense," I say, doubtful of the results. I'm not too good at any assignment that requires me to be still.

"Ah, yes. The law of attraction." My mom sips her brown

elixir. "The shit works, I'm telling you. Usually we just make it work for the wrong reasons," she says, getting comfortable. I grab a bag of Doritos from the large wicker basket on the table full of snacks. My mom's the snack queen. I walk back across the room to retrieve my notebook from my backpack and thumb through the notes involving Marty I made today at lunch. I'm concentrating so hard on her no longer being my manager I'm surprised she made it through the day. If this stuff really worked, she'd be long gone.

"So, it worked for you to write down what you wanted to happen in any given situation?" I say, reviewing my words. Damn, my handwriting is awful. I can barely make out what I've written.

"Well, yeah, but not in a positive way. I usually wrote down negative shit. Like, for example, I remember I was dating this fool in high school, and he thought he was gone play me with some chick up the block," she says, sipping her Bailey's and getting real loose. I love it when my mom tells me about her school days. I can't believe how much of the same drama we go through from generation to generation. I wonder if this happens in all families or if it's just a Williams Woman trait. "I wrote him such a nasty letter saying that I hope she would give him syphilis and make his penis fall off and all kinds of stuff."

"Did it fall off?" I say, as my phone vibrates, signaling a text. It's Jeremy, saying he'll be here in ten minutes.

"Just about. I know he got some sort of sexually transmitted disease, and it's one that will never go away. He didn't bother me again after that," my mom said, her voice low and guttural, almost frightening. I'm glad I'm not one of her enemies. I hope she's thinking about something similar happening to Ras Joe.

"So, what was negative about that?" I say. "It sounds like he got what he deserved."

"Yes, but so did the girl, and I didn't wish anything on her, not really. That's the thing about dealing with the negative side of our gifts," she says wearily. "It usually hits its target, and then some, because of the power of your intentional thoughts. When you focus a lot of passion on something, you give it energy, and that can backfire on you."

"Wow." I don't know what else to say. My mom's sitting here telling me that her thoughts made this dude catch something and pass it on to the trick he was fooling around with. That doesn't sound so bad to me. "So how exactly did you do this?" I say, ready to take notes. Maybe I can have similar residual luck with Tania but without affecting Jeremy.

That's what I'm trying to tell you; negative always hits more than the intended victim, my mom says without speaking. Damn, I still forget she can do that.

"Mom, just talk to me without reading my mind," I say. It was enough having to be careful what I say around her, now I have to be careful what I think, too.

Okay, she says, still on the telepathic plane. Seeing my frustration, my mom stops and comes back down to my level. "You have to let me practice sometimes."

"I'm actually proud of you for reclaiming your power, even if it only works on me." I wish she'd stuck with her studies, like she's advising me to do. I think my mom's very powerful in her own right, and she could use some of that power to help a sistah out.

"Well, thank you very much," she says, her green eyes glistening in the setting afternoon sun. The time recently changed, falling one hour behind, so it's starting to get dark earlier. "Learn from my mistakes, Jayd," she says, placing her empty glass on the coffee table in front of her and curling up into the fetal position, ready to sleep the rest of the day away. My phone vibrates again, indicating Jeremy's arrival.

"Is White boy here?" she says, smiling at herself. Why is everyone hating on Jeremy lately?

Because we can sense your true feelings, even without you saying them, my mom says, again not moving her lips.

"Mom, I love Jeremy." As the words slip from my mouth for the first time, I realize that they are only half true. I love a lot of things about Jeremy. But I don't have the same feeling as I did when I first felt love for Rah, which hasn't gone anywhere. Can I love more than one person at a time? I know it's more than infatuation, like I had with KJ. But when Jeremy told me he loved me, it really threw me off. Not so much because of the short amount of time we've been together, but more because if you love someone, you'll do anything for them—even if you're just friends. And that isn't how Jeremy rolls at all.

"That boy's just plain selfish, if you ask me." I don't recall asking my mom anything about him, but I need to get downstairs. I text him a message saying my mom's asleep and I will meet him at the car. "But most men are in one way or another. You'll figure out how you really feel about him in time." Here we go with this time thing again. Why can't I just know all the answers to my questions right now?

Because that would take the lessons out of life, Jayd. And that's no life at all, she communicates telepathically before drifting off. I walk over and kiss my mom's ebony cheek. Her skin's so soft and flawless. I hope I look like her when I'm in my thirties. I pick up my bags next to the couch and head out the door. As I lock the multiple locks, I remember the first time I went to Jeremy's house and saw his huge oak door with one lock. We are very different, maybe too different. But I'm still willing to give this relationship a try, no matter what others may think I think.

When I get downstairs, Jeremy's propped up against the hood of his car, casually waiting and blocking the driveway.

"What's up, babe?" he says, walking toward me and taking my bags before kissing me on the lips. He must be chewing Juicy Fruit, one of my favorite gums. Following him to the passenger's side, I get comfortable as he slides my bags into the backseat before closing my door. He's loudly playing Creed, causing the other tenants to look out their windows as if to say, "What the hell is all that noise?" If it was Ludacris or Snoop, no one would give it another thought. But the fact that it's alternative music causes heads to turn.

"Can we turn that down a little until we pull out?" I say, feeling a little self-conscious. I've never felt like this when Nigel or Rah picks me up, and their music's always hella loud. But the attention is making me feel like a target on a dartboard. Jeremy definitely can't do this when he takes me back to Mama's tonight. I'd never hear the end of it.

"Sure," he says, sitting in the driver's seat and lowering the volume before closing the door. "Is everything all right?" Jeremy looks concerned.

"Yeah. Why do you ask?" Why am I lying? I should just come out and straight ask him what I want to know. He doesn't have to know how I got my inside information. I just have to be tactful with my approach. But Jeremy's right, I'm tense and for many reasons. Not having Nellie to vibe with is really throwing me off. Even with all her princess qualities, she's still my best friend, and I miss her. Maybe if I send her a text real quick she'll hit me back.

Hey Nellie. Just checking on you. Hit me when you get this.

I send, still awaiting Jeremy's reply.

"I don't know. Lately you seem a little high-strung, like

something's bothering you," he says, feigning ignorance. He can't be serious.

"Well, for starters, your former fling has stolen my best friend away from me, and she's trying to get you back, too," I say as we back out of the driveway and head toward the beach. It's a warm evening, but as soon as the sun sets completely, the night chill will hit. I'm glad I brought my sweater—the same sweater I let Nellie borrow over the summer and she didn't get it back to me until the first day of school. That's my girl.

"Jayd, you can't let Tania get to you, I already told you that," Jeremy says, turning Creed back up, but not so loud that we can't hear each other.

"Is it really that simple?" Maybe everything in his world actually is that cut-and-dry. To have a baby on the way, he seems remarkably calm. A little too calm, if you ask me. "Why doesn't shit bother you that would worry the hell out of a normal person?" I say, realizing we're heading for Palos Verdes. "And where are you taking me?"

"Well, which question do you want me to answer first?" he says, trying to be a smart-ass, but I'm not in the mood.

"Take your pick," I say, returning his attitude tenfold.

"Well, my dad decided to have a barbecue at the last minute, so I was hoping you wouldn't mind coming back to my house for dinner instead of going out," he says, casually dropping a bomb on me. I'm in no mood to deal with his dysfunctional family today. What the hell?

"Why didn't you tell me before now!" I yell, practically drowning out the smooth tunes. How could he spring a surprise like this on me?

"Well, because I just found out when I left to come and get you," Jeremy says, not realizing how upset he's just made me. "What's the big deal?" he adds, trying to make light of the situation.

"The big deal is that you didn't tell me about it, so I'm not prepared. I'm dressed for coffee by the pier, not dinner with the family." Rah would never pull no shit like this. He would just know better. And so would KJ, for that matter. It must be a cultural thang.

"Nobody cares what you look like. My parents love you." Now, he should know both of those statements are the furthest thing from the truth. His mother's a strange wench, and his dad's always drunk, so who knows what he really thinks. But whenever I'm around them I feel like I'm on display.

"Jeremy, can we skip the social hour and just kick it, you and me?" I plea. Maybe if I'm sweet he'll let me have my way. We have too much unsettled business, and we need to be alone to discuss it all.

"Jayd, stop being so self-conscious. As quick as you are to tell people off, I'd think you could care less about what people think of you," Jeremy says, uncovering some buried resentment of his own. I knew he was embarrassed by my mouth, but I had no idea he was still upset about it.

"Are you serious?" I say, ready to go off but trying to keep my cool. "You can't be comparing you not telling me where we're going so that I would know what to expect to me getting into it with Tania the other day."

"All I'm saying is that you can't have it both ways. Either you care what people think about you or you don't." I think things are just that simple from his point of view. His crystal-blue eyes sparkle as the last of the sun hides in the horizon, allowing the evening to begin. We're almost up the hill, entering into Palos Verdes Estates. I'm sure many people envy the folks up in here. But personally, I'd rather be at home.

"Here we are," Jeremy says, pulling up to the huge lawn in front of his house. The smell of the grill makes my stomach growl, even if I may protest the whole thing. The rest of our ride was uncomfortably silent. Jeremy can be so self-righteous sometimes it drives me crazy. He thinks he knows the best way always, and that's just not so. I admit, I do have a slight temper. But keeping stuff bottled up for too long can be hazardous to your health. And a sistah can't afford any unnecessary ulcers.

"Can you pass me my sweater from the back?" I say as Jeremy exits the Mustang, walking around to my side with the sweater in tow. He can be so sweet yet such a jackass. I think I have a pattern of choosing similar boyfriends, no matter their skin tone.

"Here you go," he says, slipping the petite cardigan over my shoulders and closing the car door. There's a definite synergy between us, I'll admit. He smells so good to me all the time. And I love our conversations. But lately it seems all we ever talk about are things we disagree about. And there's more of that likely to come at the barbecue.

"Jayd," his mom says as we approach the side gate. She gives me a big hug and drags me off into the picturesque backyard. This lady must spend a fortune on her gardens alone, not to mention the cascading waterfalls, the pond and the spacious grass area, where Jeremy's brother and several other neighbors are engaged in a game of football.

"Hey, babe, I'll be right back," Jeremy says, running off toward the impromptu field and leaving me alone with his mother. Oh, I'll never forgive him for this one. Luckily I see China across the yard. She catches my eye and starts to walk over and rescue me from the shrew but not before she can get a few jabs in.

"So, Jayd, I see you're becoming acclimated to the beach crowd," Mrs. Weiner says, eyeing me like she's sizing up a slave on the auction block. This woman's energy is familiar in an ancient-evil kind of way. She reminds me a lot of Mrs. Bennett, but at least her perfume smells nicer.

"It's not hard to do," I say. The last thing I want to do is engage with this woman right now or a bunch of the rich kids from school. It seems like every family on the block is here, and there's enough food to feed a hundred more. When we have barbecues on our block, it usually means Daddy fires up the grill, one of my uncles brings the radio outside, we fill up the ice chest and there's our barbecue. These folks went out and hired a caterer, hired a deejay, set up different seating arrangements and have servers and a full bar—and this was supposedly last minute. It must be nice to live on the other side of poverty. But as Mama says, under-appreciation of one's abundance leads to idle time, and idle time is evil's playground. If she's right, then this must be their gymboree.

"Hey, Jayd," China says, carrying her small Yorkshire terrier dressed in beachwear, matching her attire perfectly. It seems I'm the only one fully clothed and without a dog. I know I'm in lala land now. The heating lamps installed throughout the space make it unnaturally warm out here, and everyone's taking full advantage of the mixed blessing.

"Hey, girl. What's up?" I say, petting her mini pooch. "Don't forget about Wednesday." I remind her of my free day from the AP meetings.

"Girl, I got you. Hi, Judy," she says, smiling at Jeremy's mother, who's now fully distracted by the now empty martini glass in her hand. No matter how much I may not like her, I would never feel comfortable calling her by her first name. I guess that's just how I was raised.

"Hello, China, dear," says, her Southern drawl now a slur.

"Jayd, let's go watch the game. My boyfriend's playing, too," China says, leading me toward the grassy area and away from Mrs. Weiner, who's now headed toward the bar for another round, joining her husband and their friends, who seem to be having a good time. I guess I can't fully blame Jeremy for being a product of his environment. I'm just not used to this version of normal.

"So what's up with your girl Nellie?" China says as we continue our arm-linked hike up the hill toward the game of shirts versus skins, where, unfortunately for me, Jeremy's still got his shirt on. Damn.

"What made you ask me that?" I say, following her eyes to the chill area. Tania, Laura, Reid, Matt, Chance and Nellie are among the bystanders on the sidelines. So, she got into their world on her own merit. I guess I should congratulate Nellie while I still have the chance, since she's not returning any of my messages or even acknowledging my presence.

"She's not acting herself lately," China says. "I asked her if you were coming, and she acted as if she didn't know you," she continues, not realizing the combustible scene running through my head I'm trying to avoid causing.

"Is that right?" I say, heading in Nellie's direction. "Well, let's see if she can ignore me now." Noticing my approach, Nellie looks uncomfortable, like me being here makes it obvious she doesn't belong. Tania, seeing Nellie's discomfort, looks up to see me in their faces again.

"Hey, girl," Chance says, not rising from his comfy spot. He's been waiting a long time to get this close to Nellie, and he ain't giving his seat up, not even to hug one of his best friends. Ain't that some shit?

"Now, now, you know Jeremy doesn't like it when you have these embarrassing tantrums in public," Tania says, sipping on her white wine. Isn't she pregnant? What's she doing drinking?

"Tania, don't talk to me. I just wanted to say hi to my girl," I say, crossing my arms and staring down at Nellie, who's stretched out across one of the dozens of lawn chairs speckled around the field. The game's still going on, and no one on the field's paying much attention to us on the sidelines. Reid's brothers are of course on the opposing team of Jeremy and his brothers, and it looks like Jeremy's ready to go back in. I know he don't want none of me right now.

"Hi, Jayd," Nellie mumbles. What the hell have I done to this girl to make her turn on me like this? It can't be that great being the token black girl around here.

"So you *do* remember me," I say, taking my vibrating phone out of my purse to see Rah's name on the caller ID. If he didn't live so far from here, I'd ask him to come get me now. "Why can't you return any of my messages?" I say, trying not to be as loud as the people around me are assuming me to be.

"I told you I've been busy. There's a lot more involved in being a princess than I thought," Nellie says, looking like she actually wants to tell me what's really going on, but she can't. Something in me tells me not to press her any further and to trust that the truth will be revealed. What the hell are they doing to my girl, and why is she letting them?

"Jayd, is everything all right?" Jeremy says, out of breath and wiping his sweaty forehead on the front of his shirt. Even now, he still smells good to me.

"Yeah, baby. I was just hollering at my friends," I say, looking from Nellie to Chance, making both of them lower their eyes in shame. How could they kick it with the enemy? Catching my eye, Tania looks at me as though she wants to say something, but she doesn't. She settles instead on a devious smile and waves her left hand in front of me, showing off the three-carat diamond ring, reminding me of her engagement. Just then, I get a flush on my arm, where the fading burn mark is. This whole episode feels too familiar, like another déjà vu. This can't be good.

"Heads up!" Jeremy's brother Justin yells from the field. With me not moving soon enough, the ball hits me in the arm, right where my wound is healing, causing the pain to once again flare up.

"Jayd, are you okay?" Jeremy says, unaware of the mark there, prior to the impending bruise sure to come. What the hell?

"Yeah, I'm fine," I say. If I didn't want to leave before, I definitely want to now.

"It's just a little hit; it'll be okay," Jeremy says. His touch is a little more than I can bear right now, even if he is trying to be sweet.

"Ouch. Don't touch it," I say, jerking my arm away from his hand. Looking pissed, Jeremy takes a step back to return to the game. Tania and her crew are enjoying this a little too much.

"You're such a baby sometimes," he says, only half joking. "You'll be all right." And with that, he returns to his game, and I march off the field, with China right behind me.

"Hey, Jayd, wait up," she says, clutching her pet tightly while speeding down the hill after me. I just want to get out of here. I'm sure I can find a bus stop somewhere and get my ass back to Compton, where I know how to play the game. This is some new territory for me, where you can flaunt your lovers in front of your current girlfriends and friends alike and everyone's supposed to be fine with that. Well, not where I'm from.

"I was just leaving. Do you want a ride home?" China says. She probably has always wanted to go to Compton.

"Sure. I just need to get my stuff out of Jeremy's car," I say as we walk toward the front. He didn't lock the doors, so I can leave unnoticed and get back to my side of town.

~ 6 ~
Fiyah

"Ay candela, candela/
Candela, me quemo aé."

—BUENA VISTA SOCIAL CLUB

Jeremy called me all night long after my dramatic exit yesterday. I didn't answer a single call, and I talked to Rah only briefly after taking a cleansing bath Mama prescribed to help calm my dreams. She said I have too much hot energy around me and I need to cool my head. She gave me some orikis to sing for my Ori, and they actually made me feel better—low spirit, sore arm and all.

This morning when Jeremy picked me up from the bus stop, he didn't speak a word to me. I tried to explain to him why I left without saying anything and why I didn't pick up the phone, but he just acted as if I weren't talking at all. I shouldn't have to continuously justify my actions. What else was I supposed to do after he called me a baby in front of my sworn enemy and best friend turned frenemy—sit there and chat it up? He's really tripping on this one.

"Jayd," Alia says, snapping me out of my recollection of this morning's events and back to my fifth-period drama class. She and Seth are rehearsing a scene from *Waiting for Godot*, and I'm supposed to cue their lines. But I'm not even paying attention to the two of them. They've been over it a hundred times, and they're both great actors. I'm sure they have the script down pat. "Wake up," she says, snatching the small playbook out of my hands and reviewing her lines.

"You studying your own lines—what a novel idea," I say, teasing her. Alia's my girl, and I am sorry I'm not being of much help to them right now, but I've got more important things on my mind.

Ever since running into Nellie yesterday, I've been getting a strange feeling that there's more to her hanging out with Tania than just wanting to be in with the popular kids. I feel like Tania's holding something over Nellie's head, and I'm going to find out what's going on. I think Jeremy should be willing to help me in any way he can. And, more than anything, he should always have my back, especially in front of an ex. That would be like me choosing sides with KJ if they got into an argument. Now, how would that look?

"Why do you look so serious?" Seth says, noticing my frown. I haven't been mentally present in any of my classes today. Jeremy got a library pass for third, and I didn't see him at lunch or break either. He's skillfully avoiding me, and I don't mind having the time to myself to think. I'm sure Tania and her baby had a hangover, because she was conveniently absent today as well. And without their queen bee, the hive is usually quite silent.

"I just have a lot going on," I say, avoiding discussing anything with Seth. Even though the Drama Club is a clique unto itself, private conversations still end up getting spread around campus. And the less people I have in my business, the better. "Did I miss a line or something?" I say, watching Alia frantically search through the worn playbook.

"Alia swears she missed an entire monologue. I think it's just her ego talking," Seth says almost as feminine as me. Alia and Seth playing the roles is almost equivalent to it being two girls onstage, instead of two men, as originally cast.

"I'm telling you, I know I had another paragraph in here

somewhere. We're off pace, and we finished two minutes early," Alia says, reminding us that the bell is about to ring. Maybe I can dance some of this stress out in sixth period. Mama has a neighborhood-watch meeting at Mrs. Webb's house up the block, so I should have plenty of time to study tonight. Those meetings last for hours, and when Mama gets home, she's worn out. It's really just a large gossip session, during which everyone finds out who's been visiting whom. And Daddy's name always manages to come up, putting Mama in a sour mood for the rest of the evening.

"There's the bell," Alia says, picking up her oversize backpack and heading toward the door. "Thanks for your help, Jayd. See you after school for rehearsal, Seth."

"All right, Alia," he says, turning his attention toward me. I'm moving real slow today. Luckily we have the first fifteen minutes to dress, so I'm never in too much of a hurry to get there.

"So, you heard about Tania's little growth, did you?" Seth says like he's been dying to dish the dirt for days. "Girl, and you know who the baby daddy is, right?" he adds a little too comfortably for me.

"No, but I'm sure you'll tell me," I say, allowing him to do all the talking. When I come to Jeremy with this information after school, I want it to be all on Seth and his gossip skills, not me. This is my perfect opportunity. He'll have to tell me something now.

"Girl, it's your boo, Jeremy. Or at least that's what the queen says." Damn, he sounds too much like a hating girl right now. Seth is one of those rich-kid outcasts. I have the feeling he's always wanted to be best friends with Tania or someone in the crew but was never allowed, and for obvious reasons. Seth's nails are much prettier than any of those girls'.

"Where'd you hear that from?" I say, feigning surprise. This is my acting assignment for the day, I guess. I'm glad

Seth came out with what he knows. It's actually a relief to have someone else to talk to about it.

"Girl, from the witch herself. I overheard Tania and Jeremy talking the other day. He wants a paternity test, and she doesn't. Tania just wants him to sign over any possible rights to claim paternity in the future and let her go on and marry the rich Persian dude her parents hooked her up with," he says. Seth sure did overhear a lot, and I'm glad, too. Now I know what Jeremy knows, and that means I can help him, whether he wants it or not. So much for having to wait until he trusted me enough to tell me. This plan's much quicker.

"Really? So she doesn't even know if he's the father?" I say. I wouldn't be dreaming about it if it weren't true. But I have to continue to play the shocked role. I don't want Seth to know I already knew. That could get back to Jeremy, and then he really wouldn't trust me.

"No, but she's pretty sure. She usually doesn't go around unprotected, know what I mean?" I think Seth knows what he means better than I do. I've heard he's been an undercover boyfriend to a couple of dudes around campus. But he's unusually discrete about his love life. "And she hasn't even met her fiancé," he says, completely enthralled with Tania's affairs. I bet if she ever becomes famous, he'll be the one to write her biography.

"Okay, Seth, that's enough of *The Young and the Restless* for today," I say, getting up to leave before the final bell rings. It's going to take me about six minutes to walk across campus to the dance studio. This school's too big for me. But all the hiking does keep me in shape. It's also a perfect warm-up before I get my groove on for the day. "I have to get to class, and so do you," I say, knowing he only has to go across the stage to his set and design course. He's a total thespian lover.

"Okay. I know this must be painful for you, Jayd, and you're still in shock," he says, "but don't kill them. You have your whole life ahead of you, and you're too pretty to go to prison." Seth exits the classroom through the door leading to the stage. He's so silly, and I'm sure he and many others would love to see me beat Tania down. But I have other tricks up my sleeve to achieve the same goal—getting her out of my life. I'm going to put all my cards on the table and tell Jeremy what I heard, but not all that I know. Judging from his reaction, I'll know the best way to go about helping him.

I practically sweated out my press-and-curl during dance class, and the cool ocean breeze feels good against my moist scalp and skin. So good, I'm not even paying attention to Misty and KJ making out on the bleachers across the field. They're disgusting, and she's just getting played, just like Nellie. Can't these girls see they're being used? They must be in complete denial because neither one of them can be that stupid. Well, Misty maybe. But definitely not Nellie. Speaking of which, I haven't seen her all day. I hope she hasn't started drinking with the rest of Tania and her disciples.

"Hey, Jayd," Chance says, walking toward the front of the school where he and Jeremy's cars are parked. "What's up with you?" He tries to make small talk after shunning me yesterday.

"What's up is that people I thought were my friends are turning out to be the shadiest ones in my life right now. That's what's up," I say, speeding up and making him jog to catch up to me. I'm not in the mood for another trifling homie right now. I know Chance doesn't mean any harm. But seriously, choosing Nellie in bitch mode over me is just plain wrong.

"Come on, Jayd, I didn't mean to hurt your feelings," he says, grabbing my arm and forcing me to stop and look him in the eye. He does look pathetically sorrowful, like a puppy who chewed up my favorite shoes.

"Even if you didn't intentionally hurt my feelings, you still did it, and that doesn't make it okay," I say, not giving in so easily.

"I know, I know. Look, I'll make it up to you," he says, taking out a coupon for Baskin Robbins. Last year he used to treat me to a sundae every time the Drama Club went out after a play. He always has a buy-one-get-one-free coupon, and I can never resist.

"Okay," I say. "But now you owe me one." And I intend for him to pay up.

"You know you can't stay mad at your big bro," he says, putting his arm around my neck and walking me toward the front where I can see Jeremy waiting by his Mustang. He still looks like he's in a foul mood. "Besides, can you blame a guy for getting close to his future wifey?" Chance is delirious if he thinks Nellie will ever get with him.

"Whatever, Chance," I say, quickly shifting gears before Jeremy is within earshot. "How long have you known about Tania's pregnancy?" Chance looks down at me, sizing me up to see how much I know. He knows me well enough to know when I'm fishing for information. He wouldn't break last time I asked him what was up with Jeremy and Tania. But now that I'm on the in, he's got to give a little.

"Who told you about that?" he says, stalling. "I know it wasn't Jeremy."

"No, it wasn't, and that's irrelevant," I say, impatient with his reverse grilling. "Why are you being so secretive with me?" I use the sweetest voice I've got. If I could gauge how Jeremy's dealing with the whole situation from a male perspective, I may have better luck in my approach. But Chance is wasting time, and we are almost at his car, which is right next to Jeremy's.

"Because, Jayd, this isn't really about you. It's about them. And as a good friend to my boy, I can't talk about it with you, per his request," Chance says.

"Well, I just hope he's as loyal to you as you are to him," I say, releasing myself from his grasp. Where are my loyal-to-the-end friends? I think Mickey's the closet thing I've got to it, now that Nellie's tripping. But I think Mickey would choose a dude over me if it came down to it, just like Chance did with Nellie.

"He is. We've known each other since elementary school; we're like brothers, Jayd. Don't be mad, girl," he says, again reaching for my neck. But I don't want him touching me right now. He's taking his loyalty to Jeremy too far this time.

"Whatever," I say as we approach the cars. Jeremy still looks hella pissed at me. But now I could care less. The info is out there, and I want him to know that I know.

"So what's this about you being Tania's baby daddy?" I say with one hand on my hip while the other swings my backpack into the open passenger's door. "And no, sonny, Tubs didn't rat you out. I heard it through the beach vine." Jeremy looks from a stunned Chance back to me, completely emotionless. I can't read him at all.

"It is what it is," Jeremy says, as stoic as ever. That's all he has to say? What the hell kind of reaction is that? He can't be serious.

"That's all you have to say to me? Why didn't you tell me?" I say, now practically shouting, which is having the opposite affect on him as I hoped.

"Because I'd knew you'd react like this," Jeremy says, walking around to his side and getting in. "Later, Chance," he adds, starting the car.

"Later, dude. And, Jayd, don't stay mad at me for long. I still love you, girl," Chance says before getting into his car and pulling off, leaving me to deal with Jeremy on my own.

"Are you coming?" he says. I'm not used to dealing with aloof guys. This isn't the way I imagined this conversation going at all. I thought he'd come clean and tell me everything. I want the details.

"Yeah," I say, getting in and shutting the door. He pulls

away from the curb before I even have a chance to put on my seatbelt. "Are you going to talk to me about this?"

"No," he says. And that's that. At least when I busted Rah and KJ, they came clean and were sympathetic. This fool's acting like he could care less. The ride home is destined to be a quiet one, just like the ride to school this morning. Without him to talk to and Mama at her meeting tonight, I guess I'll have plenty of time to get my assignments straight for the week. I also need to put some energy on finding out what's exactly up with Nellie. Maybe I should talk to Ms. Toni when she gets back from her leader's conference on Wednesday. I guess I'll have to wait and talk to Mama tomorrow after school. Maybe she'll have some better ideas than just writing stuff down. Now's the time to take action.

"Girl, I tell you what you need to do with that little friend of yours," Netta says, clanking the hot flatiron in the air, ready to run it through Mama's half-pressed hair. It's Mama's standing Tuesday appointment, also the best time to catch her at her wisest, other than when she's cooking. "You tell her the next time some mess goes down, you won't be there for her. Where do you find your friends, girl? At the enemy surplus store?" she says, turning Mama's chair around so it faces me.

With Jeremy not talking to me and Mickey sneaking off campus with Nigel every chance she gets, school has become less fun lately and I've been getting more homework done at school than usual, leaving my afternoons free to study my spirit work and talk to Rah. Last night we got to talk for a few minutes before I went to bed. He's supposed to call me tonight, but I'm trying to be good. It's too easy to give in to temptation when things get difficult in relationships. Mickey and Nigel are the perfect example.

"You and your mama have a knack for attracting the

wrong kind of friends," Mama says, her eyes closed as she holds her head back, allowing Netta to get as close to her scalp as possible.

"My mom has real tight friends," I say, referring to her homegirls, my aunt Vivica being the closest of them all.

"Yeah, but she's also had some real terrible friends, too."

"So have you, Lynn Mae. Girl, you could write a book talking about all the haters you had around you back in the day, and still. Girl, women in the church used to pretend to be your mama's friend just so they could get close to your daddy," Netta says, giving up the good dirt, as usual. "Jayd, your mama used to have more women around her than men back in those days. Now they know better, and so does your mama here." Mama is surprisingly quiet during Netta's tale. Usually she'd be trying to shut her up.

"Mama, is she right?" I ask, sitting straight up in the drier chair across from Netta's station. I wonder what it's like when her other clients are here. It's always empty on Tuesdays.

"Unfortunately, Jayd, yes, she is. Some people try to be your friends just so they can get something out of you. And those friends are the worst kind of enemies to have because they know you well." Mama looks unusually weary. This is one of her busiest times of the year, and I know she's tired of dealing with the church folk. And after last night's block-club meeting, I'm sure she's had enough of them to last her for quite a while. Daddy and her have barely spoken two words to each other since she went off on him about some late-night phone call from God knows who. When Mama gets home, I'm sure she'll just want to get in her bed.

"You sound just like my mom in my dream a couple of weeks ago," I say, recalling my mother's warning about friends turning into leaches—or frenemies, as she calls them.

"Yes, Jayd. Sometimes it takes multiple great minds to come together to accomplish a goal," Mama says, opening her eyes and looking straight through me. "If you want Nellie back as your friend, you're going to have to stop going at it alone. Where's Mickey at in all this?" she says, bringing up a good point. Mickey's closer to Nellie than Mickey is to me, and she's acting like the girl doesn't even exist. Mama's right. Me and Mickey need to get our friend back and away from Tania's drunken clutches. I can't do it alone.

"She's too busy running after Nigel," I remind her.

"Oh, that girl's weaving a tangled web," Mama says. "That gangster boyfriend of hers didn't just fall off the dumb truck yesterday. I hope she knows what she's getting into." Mama rises from her seat, indicating she's ready to go. Netta whipped her French twist up so fast, if I didn't know better I'd say it was magic.

I don't think any of us knows what we're getting into at the beginning of any relationship, because it all feels so good. The smiles and giggles, the first kiss, the text messages and all-night conversations; there's even a rush when you and your girls hit it off for the first time, like you found your tribe. But now I feel like I'm alone on *Survivor* without a rope to swing from. And Mickey could care less about anyone but herself right now. I'll just have to make her come around to seeing things my way.

"Reality sucks sometimes, and we all have to deal with it, Jayd," Mama says as we both hug Netta good-bye before heading out the neon-lit door. "You can't live in a fantasy world forever, and neither can your girls. Focus on the outcome and you can change your present circumstances." She's right. I just have to get Nellie to see that the people around her are a bunch of fakes and that if she's not careful, she's going to end up just like them. And if that happens, I won't be able to help her at all because if it's one thing I can't stand, it's a fake.

~ 7 ~
Fake

"Why are you such a fake?"

—THE BRAND NEW HEAVIES

Since Mama took it down early tonight, I have the spirit room all to myself to study. It's packed in here with dozens of Mama's spirit bags for her Halloween clients and the regulars. I found a couple of unmarked bags in the cabinet next to the spirit book. I wonder who they're for.

"Lexi, you scared me," I say to our German shepherd, who is walking into the room through the small doggy door in the screen and is almost smiling, like she understands what I'm saying; most of the time, I think she can. It's weird to say, but I think Lexi's eyes are human. I don't even know if that's possible. But if it is, then she's definitely got a pair.

"Well, since you're here, you might as well help me find something to help everyone else come off their high horses and act right," I say. I realize that's a tall request for one quick potion, but I need something to work, and fast. I want to take advantage of having both break and lunch free tomorrow. Jeremy won't be able to take me home, so I've got to get to him early. And, knowing him, it may take all day for him to come around to seeing things my way.

"What, you don't think I can do it?" Now, I know the dog's not in my head, too. Everyone's got an opinion about how I should handle my relationships. But I've got to start listening to myself, and I'm telling me it's time to take some aggressive action—now.

"Here we go," I say, turning to the oils, incense and remedies portion of the book. I've never been all the way back here before. There's also a story about Maman Marie and how she used an intoxicatingly sweet scent called "sweet essence" to make everyone agree with her when she needed to resolve an issue.

"Now, this sounds like what I need," I say as Lexi plops down on the floor, ready to watch me do my thing. I think she gets a kick out of me trying to be like Mama. I hope one day I can work it like her. But until then, my mimicking will have to do.

"It says that Maman had a legal issue with the courts in Louisiana, saying she didn't report all her income and owed them in back taxes and that she thought her business partner turned enemy was the one who snitched on her. Now, that's the kind of friend no one needs." Lexi barks in agreement as I continue reading.

"It says here to mix a little Egyptian musk oil, some honey, my favorite sweet perfume, five white rose petals and a few drops of spring water." Doesn't sound too difficult, and I think Mama has all these ingredients here except for my favorite perfume, Escada's Rockin' Rio, which I left at my mom's house. If I keep it here, I'm likely to never see it again with all the sticky fingers around. I'll just have to use whatever perfume Mama has in the house.

"Now all I need is something to put all this in," I say as I continue looking through the cramped cabinets for extra materials. There are mason jars in various sizes, all kinds of glass containers, woven bags, cut material, twine and other methods of storing and distributing Mama's products. She keeps it simple and effective—just like her clients like it.

"Here we go," I say, finding the container full of small

glass vials with matching droppers. "This should do the trick. It says here this scent is attractive to anyone who gets a whiff, instantly making them more pliable, and that's exactly what I need all my friends to be right now. Jeremy's unreasonable cold, Mickey's being selfish and Nellie's just plain tripping. It's time for everyone to get on my side so we can all get Tania out of the way. Tomorrow morning I'll start with Jeremy and work on Mickey next. With the two of them working with me, I know I can get Nellie away from the dark side and back to being the brat we know and love."

After the long bus rides to school this morning, the last thing I'm in the mood for is to be kept waiting, and that's exactly what's happening now. Jeremy has never left me waiting at the bus stop, and he's not picking up his phone. What the hell? Just when I begin to walk up the hill toward campus, he pulls up.

"Hey, sorry I'm late. Overslept," he says, looking unusually groggy.

"Are you feeling okay?" I say, getting into the car and feeling his forehead. I'm not sure what I'm feeling for, but if cold and clammy means he's sick, then he needs a doctor right now. "What's going on?"

"I don't know," he says as I close the door. "I woke up with a scratchy throat this morning. And after my surf—"

"I don't mean to cut you off, but what do you mean after your surf? You still got in some cold-ass water and you already weren't feeling well?" I know I sound more like his mama than his girlfriend, but really, he can't be that stubborn.

"Damn, Jayd, do you know how not to react to anything?" he says, truly annoyed. It's a bright morning, and everyone's enjoying the warm sun. People are watering their lawns and walking their dogs, living carefree while I suffocate in his car.

"Why do I feel like I'm always on the defense with you?" At first, his witty mind is what attracted me to him. But now it's pissing me off.

"You don't have to be anything you don't want to be," he says, turning into the crowded parking lot at the front of our school. The red and white letters spell out SOUTH BAY HIGH, CALIFORNIA DISTINGUISHED SCHOOL on the marquee, but it really should read DRAMA HIGH. "You're a really defensive person," he says, putting me again on the stand. But I'm not the one on trial here; Jeremy is.

"What do you mean, I'm defensive?" I say, this time without raising my voice. I think Maman's sweet-essence perfume isn't having much of an effect on him because he's congested. Damn, I should've stuck with the cupcakes. Even though they don't come out perfect, they still get the job done. He expertly parks in one of the tight spaces and turns off the engine. Jeremy takes a deep breath in and one out, turning to look me in the eye. I've never seen him look so serious, not even when he was busted for selling weed on campus.

"Jayd, look, I love your fire just as much as the next guy, hopefully more," Jeremy says, slightly smiling and revealing his straight white teeth. God, this boy is adorable. Why does he have to be such an ass? "But I can't take this drama every day."

"What drama?" I say. I know he's not talking about my attitude toward Tania, because that girl deserves all the attitude I've got to give and more.

"What drama? Are you kidding?" he says, amused by my question. "You always have some issue with someone around you. First it was KJ and his girl, and then it was Misty, now it's Nellie and Tania. Why can't you let some shit slide?" There's that mellow beach attitude I don't get.

"Yeah, Jeremy, right," I say, grabbing my backpack from my lap and opening the door. I need some air. I think this perfume's having more of an influence on me than it is on him. I can't get riled up at him, no matter what he says. I want to, but I just smell too good to get hot.

"I know you think it's not that easy, Jayd, but it is. You don't always have to control everything. Just let people be," Jeremy says, exiting the car with me. He grabs his backpack from the backseat before closing his door and walking around to my side.

"Is that what you're doing with Tania, just letting her and your baby be?" I say. Any other day that wouldn't have come out as nice as it did just now. Maybe I needed to read the whole story to see how this scent really works.

"Look, baby, the thing is," he says, pausing to find the right words while putting his arms around my waist; I miss being close to him and I miss the way he smells up close, "I didn't want to hurt you, and I know how vicious Tania can be." I look up into his blue eyes and see some of the truth but not all. He's still hiding something, but what? Lying is the same thing as faking to me. So if he doesn't come clean soon, we're going to have some issues, and no amount of perfume will help me chill.

"I can handle Tania," I say as the first bell of the day rings. "You have to learn to trust me." I accept his gentle kiss. Now that's more like it.

"I do trust you," he says, but I can hear the apprehension in his voice. What else is going on he doesn't want me to know about? "But sometimes you're going to have to let me trust when to tell you things." He's right but only to a certain extent. This boy's got a twisted version of how to react to vital situations. He's right about me having a lot of action around me and me wanting to control it. But what am I supposed to do? Just watch while people's worlds fall apart all around me? No, not me.

Speaking of which, I've got to get Mickey to help me with

Nellie. Jeremy can call me a controlling person if he wants to, but if I can see a solution to a problem, I'd be a fool not to try.

My first two periods were uneventful, and Mrs. Malone accepted my portfolio, just as I thought. China was in class and let me know she had my back for the AP meetings, leaving me free to launch mission "Rescue Nellie." I know Mickey and Nigel will probably be posted up on a bench in the Senior Quad, so that's where my mission begins. She's been completely unreceptive to helping our girl out, but hopefully she'll get a whiff of my scent and change her mind.

"Mickey, we need to talk," I say, snatching her up by the arm and marching her toward the Main Quad, away from her comfy bench with Nigel. I'm almost more sick of the two of them than I am of Misty and KJ. But today they're not making my stomach curl as they usually do.

"Damn, Jayd, what's got your panties in such a bunch?" she says, taken a little off guard at me being so rough with her. But I know she wasn't going to just leave her lip-lock with Nigel on her own accord.

"Look, I'm tired of you acting like Nellie doesn't exist," I say, immediately causing her to roll her hazel contacts.

"Nellie who?" Mickey says, turning around to return to her comfy bench. But not so fast. I'm not leaving until I get the answer I came for.

"Mickey, don't be like that. She's your girl," I say, ready to plead my case as sweetly as possible. But if this doesn't work, I'm going to have to put my foot where it doesn't belong to get my point across.

"Was my girl. I don't know who that chick is," she says, pointing her finger toward the Main Quad where the athletes, cheerleaders and ASB members are sitting. The Halloween Masquerade Ball is starting to create a buzz around campus, and I'm sure they're all planning the affair, Nellie apparently included. "I don't deal with fakes, Jayd, and my real girls know that."

"Look, there's more going on than just your girl wanting to switch cliques," I say, hell-bent on getting through to her. As much as I hate to admit it, Mickey's right. At first glance, it looks like our girl has sold her soul to the devil. But I know she's just faking it. Nellie's still our girl inside. "They're holding something over her head, and I need you to help me get through to her. She needs to know we've still got her back; it's the only way to help her."

"Are you kidding me?" she says, looking from Nellie to me and back to Nigel. "I've got better things to do than deal with some broad who doesn't want to be my friend anymore." She looks ready to return to her illustrious affair. But I've got one more trick up my sleeve.

"You owe me, Mickey," I say, stopping her in her tracks.

"Jayd, come on. Do you really want to use your payback for her?" I can admit that Nellie's difficult and a bit hard to take most of the time. But she's a good friend, and I can't leave her to the wolves. She'll never survive.

"At least help me prove that Tania and Reid were behind the locker-room video of Nellie, please," I say. Nigel's looking impatient, and so is Mickey.

"Why? She won't believe us no matter what we do. She's too blinded by the White green, Jayd; we can't get her into the same circles as her new friends." For the first time, I can sense Mickey's pain. Nellie hurt her, and she's angry. Why isn't she being real about how she really feels about it?

"Mickey, if you're mad at Nellie, then confront her. She probably thinks you don't care about her anymore," I say, noticing Nellie looking our way. Our eyes lock, and now I know she misses us like we do her. So why doesn't she just come clean and ditch the bitch crew?

"I don't care. As far as I'm concerned, I don't know anyone named Nellie," Mickey says, walking away for good. This isn't the way I planned this at all. What am I going to do about the two of them? A couple of weeks ago, we were as tight as my seventh-grade jeans. But now my two best friends are enemies and my boyfriend's no help. Maybe if I can talk to Nigel at lunch, he can help me convince Mickey not to leave our friend out in the cold. Maybe by then my perfume will absorb more into my skin and work a little better, because I'm not satisfied with the results. Maybe it's not working as well because I used Mama's perfume instead of my own. I'm going to have to ask her about it when I get home.

Jeremy and I didn't get to talk much because there was a movie in third period and fourth was just as boring. All I could think about was how I was going to get Mickey on my side, and I think Nigel is the best way to do that. I know the two of them hang out on the football field with the rest of the players and their groupies. I'm not giving them any peace until I get my way. I brought my sweet essence with me and dabbed some more behind my ears and on my wrist, just like Mama taught me. I hope this does the trick.

"What's up, lovebirds?" I say, sitting down on the grass next to Mickey and Nigel, momentarily ceasing their make-out session. "We've got only about twenty more minutes, so listen up and get on board if you want to continue searching for each other's tonsils," I say, making both of them laugh and pay attention.

"What's on your mind, Lady J?" Nigel says. He knows me

well enough to know when I'm not going away. Mickey just looks annoyed, like she already knows what I'm going to say.

"I need your help with Nellie," I say, setting Mickey off. There she goes, rolling her eyes again.

"What the hell, Jayd? Why do you care so much?" she yells.

"Because she's our friend and we know how friends can be sometimes," I say, directing my intention toward Nigel, who seems to be listening. "If you started tripping on Rah, would he just let you go off into the enemies' hands, or would he fight you because y'all are down like that?" I know how strong his loyalty is to our boy.

"She does have a good point, Mickey," he says, twirling her Korean hair around his finger. Mickey's the expert when it comes to hair pieces. "I don't know y'all like that," Nigel says. It seems like he's been here forever when it's only been a few weeks. "But if she's really your girl, you can't just let her go like that. You gotta knock sense into your homies sometimes; that's what we're here for, right, Jayd?" Oh, I know he's not using this as a platform to dis Jeremy. He's been rooting for Jeremy and I to break up from jump and for Rah and I to get back together. But he's losing focus from the mission at hand.

"Yes, you're right. We need to get Nellie away from those fake-ass people and knock some sense into her big head," I say, ready for the throw down. I feel very optimistic about the outcome of a confrontation; must be a side effect of my new scent.

"Whatever. I say leave the wannabe White girl to her new crowd. She's obviously made her choice. Now let her live with it." Damn, I didn't know my girl was so cold.

"Mickey, you don't mean that," Nigel says, kissing the back of her neck. If I didn't know any better, I'd think they were really falling in love.

"Yes, I do. But if ya'll are so serious about saving the wench, I guess I'll be down, too, because I am a good friend, no matter what y'all think," Mickey says, slightly melting.

"I knew you'd give in," I say, giving her and Nigel a big hug. "Now I'll leave y'all two alone. I'm going to find my man," I say, looking at my cell, which reveals ten more minutes left in the lunch period. Jeremy has a meeting after school, so if I want to see him, now's my only chance.

"He's not here," Nigel says, cutting me a smile. "Can't no White man ever love all of you, girl. That's like saying those folks will actually accept Nellie into their clique. It just ain't gonna happen." I hate to admit it, but Nigel's right; I've got to give him this one. But I'm still going to give my man the benefit of the doubt, no matter what the haters say.

~ 8 ~
Oreos

"And this is for all the Oreos/
Here's what they really think of you."

—ICE CUBE

Mama always looks so calm when she's cooking in the kitchen. I could smell the fried chicken, steamed cabbage and hot-water cornbread all the way from the bus stop. I'm still feeling optimistic about Nellie's intervention, but the whole Jeremy and Tania thing's going to require me to be a little savvier. Maybe I've been approaching this whole situation from the wrong angle. In my initial dream, it was Tania and I who talked; Jeremy was nowhere around. I wonder how open she would be if I questioned her about the baby and her intentions with Jeremy. She's probably dying to rub it in my face.

"Hey, baby. How was your day at school?" Mama says, dusting the cornmeal and flour from her freshly polished nails. She must've gotten them done today. Mama always looks fly.

"It was cool," I say, plopping down in a kitchen chair with my backpack still on. I'm exhausted, and I have a lot of homework to do, not to mention I need to return Rah's phone calls from earlier.

"Uh-oh, I know that voice," she says, sitting opposite across the kitchen table. Lexi's napping under Mama's chair, her heavy breathing providing a soothing soundtrack to our tête-à-tête.

My uncles and Jay are in the backyard playing spades, and Daddy's at church, leaving me and Mama alone to chat. "What's on your mind, little Jayd?"

"Well, I read about Maman Marie using the sweet-essence perfume to make her enemies more agreeable, but it didn't work like I expected it to," I say.

Mama looks both amused and disappointed. "What happened?" She crosses one of her legs over the other, revealing her immaculately pedicured toes. I don't understand why Daddy would want to be with another woman when he has a queen like my mother at home. But who knows what men really want.

"Instead of working on my friends, it seemed to have more of an impact on me. I mean, don't get me wrong, I still accomplished a lot, but it wasn't as easy as it should've been. I did make a substitution, using your perfume instead of mine. Could that be the reason why it wasn't as powerful?"

"Jayd, you sound like a five-year-old upset because she broke the knobs on her Etch A Sketch, and now she's wondering why it doesn't work anymore." Damn, Mama can be brutal sometimes. "I told you it's not magic, little girl. All these recipes are tools to help us, not potions to trick people into doing what you want them to do."

"Mama, I know that," I say, ready to defend myself. Maybe Jeremy was onto something when he said I was defensive. But I'll never admit that to him, no matter how good I smell. "But I just want my friends to be more pliable."

"Jayd, if you'd read the entire story, you would have known that Maman's sweet-essence perfume works because it makes the user feel more confident in what she expects, not because it tricks people into following her way." Well, that explains a lot. "You have to stop trying to control every outcome with a formula." Did she talk to Jeremy today? What the hell is up with them being in agreement about my control issues? "Again, Jayd, concentrate on the outcome you want and watch it unfold. If you are ever going to master your powers, you have to trust in your ability to change your environment without trying to manipulate others. That's where the real magic lies."

"But what's the use of knowing all this if I can't use it on others?" I say.

"Jayd, these lessons are for us and to help others through our gifts, not just manifest our personal wills." And with that last comment, Mama leaves me alone to indulge myself in her wholesome dinner and residual wisdom. I have to concentrate more on changing myself than others. And by focusing on how I want things to be, I just might be able to get the hang of that trick before I talk with Tania. It'll have to wait until Friday because I've got three tests and a paper to hand in before then. And schoolwork definitely comes before all the drama.

After Wednesday's semisuccessful attempt to get Mickey to act right, she quickly retreated from her commitment later that night on the phone when Nigel wasn't around and dodged me all day yesterday with much success. Jeremy and I made a date at break for after school, so I need to take advantage of having Mickey's ear now that it's lunch. Today I'm confident I'll get her on my side once and for all, even if I don't smell as sweet without my scented potion.

"Y'all should come to the game tonight," Nigel says, forgetting Mickey and I don't attend Westingle. It's Friday, and Jeremy's taking me to my mom's after school, as usual. "You two should come see how we get down on the west side."

"Whatever," Mickey says, rolling her eyes at the thought of venturing down the 105. Compton and Inglewood don't mix. It's only about a thirty-minute drive, but they seem worlds away. "You don't even play for them anymore," Mickey says, proving my case without me having to say a word.

"Come on. It'll be fun, I promise," he says, pulling Mickey closer into his lap. If they were sitting any closer on that bench they'd be Siamese twins.

"Well, y'all, have fun. I've got better things to do than go to a football game at somebody else's school," I say, squatting on the grass next to their bench. It's a warm, breezy day, and everyone's in the Main Quad. The athletes and cheerleaders and ASB, including the homecoming court, just announced the theme for this year's ball: the 1970s. Every year it's something different. Last year it was the American Renaissance. I started to go as a slave but opted out of showing up at all. I'd just returned from my breast surgery and didn't want to cause any more gossip than my extended absence already had. This year I might consider going, just to protect Nellie. I know something's going to go down; I can feel it in my bones.

"You have to come, too," Nigel says, smiling at me. "You know your boy's going to be there and has requested you keep your girl here company. You can't let her be the only representative of your crew." What crew? I feel more solo than ever at this school. First I befriended Misty, who turned on me, and now this madness with Nellie. And Mickey kicking it with my ex-boyfriend's best friend is just a little too much for me right now. This bull needs to end, and me going to a Westingle game where more hating broads are bound to be is out of the question.

"Nope, sorry. I already have plans," I say. I'm looking forward to hanging out at the mall with Jeremy later. My gold bangle slips down my arm, reminding me of how much I've missed spending time with Jeremy.

"With the White boy," Nigel says. He and Mickey both laugh at the fact that I have a date with my man.

"Why is it so funny that I'm going out with my boyfriend? You two aren't even together and you make more plans than any couple I know," I say, telling the truth.

"That's Black love, baby girl," Nigel says, giving Mickey a kiss while everyone in South Central stares at them. I know they're talking shit. But because it's the new quarterback and the Black girl equal only to Shae in fierceness, nobody's going to say too much about them. I think Nellie has something she wants to say; she's eyeing the lovebirds from across the yard. Rising from her seat at the ASB table, she heads our way. Perfect. Now we can get down to the business at hand: snapping Nellie back to Black and fast.

"So, you two are still just friends, right?" Nellie says, with her entourage right behind her. Tania and Laura look like they love this. Chance, Matt and Jeremy, walking across the yard to go to their cars, notice the impending drama and turn around to head our way. Damn, I don't need Jeremy thinking I'm causing more shit. He's just got to recognize there's drama in this Black girl's life and the lives of her homies.

"Nellie," Mickey asks, looking around as if she hears a voice but sees no one. "Is that you?"

Nigel laughs a little but stops when he sees my hard look. This isn't the time for jokes. Nellie has never fronted Mickey like this before, and she must be a damned fool if she thinks her new friends have got her back against Mickey. Ain't no way in hell Tania or Laura would take Mickey on. Reid doesn't even want a piece of her, not to mention her man. Just because Mickey and Nigel have sidekicks doesn't mean they aren't still loyal to each other when it comes down to business. Every time her man's on lockdown, Mickey's right there.

And when her mouth gets her into trouble, he's always got her back. That ain't the case with Nellie and her new crew.

"Don't play coy with me, Mickey," Nellie says, sounding more like a White girl than our bougie Compton sistah. What the hell have they done to her? "You're such a little liar," she adds, giving Mickey, Nigel and the rest of South Central a good laugh. Jeremy, Matt and Chance are standing behind the onlookers, patiently waiting to see what happens.

"You're such a little liar—oh, my God," Mickey says, mimicking Nellie's beach-girl accent with perfect pitch and a lot of venom. "Shut the hell up talking to me you little Oreo," Mickey says, turning her attention back to Nigel's lips. Chick drama doesn't faze him at all. Like KJ, he's used to it because it comes with the territory of being an athlete. I wonder if Nigel still gets this kind of love at Westingle?

"You were never my friend," Nellie says, egged on by the eyes of her puppet master; Tania looks like she's enjoying watching the Black girls tear at each other. Makes her job as a hater much easier, I assume. But she's not going to get away with this—not on my watch.

"Okay, Nellie, that's enough," I say, rising from my comfy spot on the grass to check my girl. "Mickey's always had your back even when you show your ass, just like now."

"This doesn't concern you, Jayd, and I didn't ask for your help," Nellie says. "You need to learn to mind your own business." Oh, no, this trick didn't just try to check me, and I'm attempting to save her narrow behind. Maybe I should let Mickey have a go at her. I'm sure Nellie would come around after a couple of slaps from Mickey's acrylic claws.

"What did you just say to her?" Mickey says, rising from Nigel's lap and stepping into Nellie's face. "You need to get over yourself, because Jayd's the only reason I haven't checked your ass properly until now." Oh, shit. All any of us needs is another detention on our records. And with all of Mickey's recent absences, I'm sure she'll be expelled after one more incident. I can't let my girls go down like this. But I've got to be smart so I don't get pulled down with them.

"God, Mickey, you're just so ghetto. How could anyone with good taste ever choose you over me?" Nellie says, rolling her eyes and turning her head away in disgust. Oh, this girl's just too much. Tania has completely changed my girl from a quasi-princess to a full-on bitch in a matter of weeks. Now, that's magic.

"Now just a minute," Nigel says, standing up to grab Mickey's charging body and stepping in front of her, confronting Nellie himself. "I think Mickey's the finest girl up here, and I have damned good taste, if I do say so myself." KJ, Misty, Del and Shae laugh. Tony and C Money look too faded to even know what's really going on. Chance, on the other hand, looks like he wants to come to Nellie's defense. But after catching my eye, he knows better than to intervene. Nellie's way off, and she deserves to get roasted; even Jeremy looks like he agrees with me for once.

"Whatever," Nellie says, turning away from the teasing crowd. " Nigel, you don't know what you're getting into with her. You're both trifling cheaters, and I hope you get caught." This gives me chills. Mama says wishing things on people with full intention can actually manifest. I think Nellie's done just that.

"You better not be threatening me," Mickey says, stepping around Nigel, only to be stopped again by his muscular arm. Luckily Nigel's a big dude, weighing at least two hundred pounds with his six-foot frame, and can easily keep Mickey from attacking Nellie, who looks completely unfazed by Mickey's anger, which proves this girl's completely lost her mind. She, better than anyone, knows what Mickey's capable of, having been her road dog for the past two years. As best friends, they know all of each other's business, which is also why best friends make the worst enemies. But even as an enemy, Nellie should know better than to push Mickey. What's gotten into this girl?

"And what if I am?" Nellie says, and Nigel can't hold her back any longer. Pushing me out of her way with one hand and reaching around Nigel with the other, Mickey starts swinging, and it's on.

"Fight! Fight!" Shae yells, causing the multiple people and seagulls around the quad to head toward the scene. As Mickey throws the first blow, Chance swoops in and grabs Nellie, taking the hit for her.

"Damn," KJ says, expressing everyone's sentiment. Mickey wears hella gold jewelry, big rings included, and cut the side of Chance's eye with one of her blinging diamonds. "That's going to leave a scar." KJ *would* be concerned with vanity. I'm glad I'm not with that fool anymore. I see what he's done to Misty's spirit. He would've never had that kind of control over me.

"Oh, shit," Mickey says, holding her hands over her mouth, truly sorry about hitting Chance, who's still in shock. "Why did you get in my way?" Mickey seems more upset that she missed Nellie's face than about catching Chance's eye. What can I say? That's my girl, and Chance is my boy. They both are being true to themselves right now. It's Nellie's who's out of order. Jeremy, sensing my need for support, comes over and grabs my backpack from the ground next to where we're all standing. Tania and her crew look bored, now that the blood has shed and it wasn't the right face.

"Nellie, you've gone too far with your little melodrama," I say, ready to leave the scene and tend to my boy's head. Chance's blood has dripped all over his white Ecko shirt, and I know that pisses him off. He spends more on his gear than the average person spends on a new car, I'm sure. Stan and Dan have arrived at the scene but too late to help. The final bell is ringing, and the crowd is dispersing. I guess the first bell rang some time ago, but no one heard it due to all the hissing going on.

"Chance didn't have anything to do with this, and you see how he got hurt?" I say, still not getting through to Nellie.

"I didn't hit him—she did," Nellie says, pointing at a still fuming Mickey, who looks like she wants to charge again. Stan and Dan look confused; then, seeing the situation, they walk away. They won't get involved if it's a girl hitting a guy.

"Watch your back, Nellie!" Mickey yells from across the yard as Nigel practically drags her away against her will. "I'm not through with you. Remember, I know shit, too, Nellie." Mickey's ready to divulge some not-so-friendly secrets of her own. "Two can play this game, Nellie, but only one of us will win." Finally Nellie's fear is sinking into her big-ass head. She's just made an enemy out of the best friend she had on this campus—probably in her entire world, other than me. But Mickey's more dangerous because she can be ruthless and cold—two streaks I don't have in blood.

"Don't listen to her," Tania says, reassuring Nellie that she did the right thing, which is the stupidest thing I've heard all day.

"Nellie, I know you still don't think they have your back, do you? They didn't say a word the whole time," I say. I can't help myself. I have to say something. Jeremy looks like he's again disappointed in my choice to speak up. Oh, well. He should've checked this broad before I was forced to handle Tania. I have visualized very clearly the end result I want to see happen—as far as Tania's concerned. According to my dream, she's supposed to be moving. Now it's up to me to make sure the elimination process takes place as quickly as possible.

"Some friends know when to shut up," Nellie says, rolling her eyes at me and following her queen bee back to the hive.

Shell-shocked, I allow Jeremy to pull me away toward drama class. I don't know how we got to this point. Where does Nellie come off turning on us like this and telling me I don't know when to shut up? She and Jeremy sound like best friends more than we do. I wish I could get Tania alone for just five minutes. That's all I need to weed this poisonous vine out of our yard.

"You all right, babe?" Jeremy says, opening the front door to my classroom well after the bell has rung. Luckily Mrs. Sinclair rarely takes roll on time, if she's even here. "You didn't have a word to say during the entire seven minutes it took to walk down here. That's a record for you," Jeremy says, trying to make me smile. But that stung a little, too.

"Am I really that bad?" I ask, seeking some sort of validation.

"Yes, but it's cute most of the time. Just lately it seems like I see so much of the fiery Jayd and less of the cool Lady J," he says, following me into the buzzing room, our teacher missing in action. "I miss her very much. See you after school." Jeremy bends down and gives me a kiss before handing me my backpack and heading out the door to his own class. It must be nice to be privileged around here.

"Are you okay?" I say, walking over to Chance, who beat us here by a few minutes. Alia has promptly taken out the first-aid kit, coming to the aid of her man—in her eyes. She's much better fit for someone as nice as he is. Nellie would wear his ass out in a week. I hope he sees that now, even with his bloodied vision.

"I'm cool. But you need to check your girl, though. She gives people like Mr. Weiner fuel for their fire," Chance says, alluding to what I don't know. But I agree, Nellie does need to check herself.

"Well, I've been trying to get through to her. You still being in her fan club hasn't helped much either. I hope you've come around to seeing things my way," I say, taking a seat next to him as Mrs. Sinclair walks in, heading straight for her office in the back, her unfinished lunch in hand. She's such a trip.

"Not Nellie," Chance says, sitting up straight in his chair, ruining Alia's fantasy of playing his nursemaid. "I'm talking about your girl Mickey. I mean, your little temper is kinda feisty and cute," he says, sounding a lot like Jeremy, "but all that anger and punching people and shit has got to go."

What the hell? "You must've gotten hit harder than I thought. You sure you don't want to go to the nurse's office?" I ask. This fool's lost his mind if he thinks Mickey was in the wrong.

"No, but maybe you do if you think Mickey punching Nellie was cool. That's just some uncalled-for bullshit, Jayd. And you know I'm right. You'd never do that to your girl, and there's a reason: because you've got class," he says. Now, see, White folks say some stupid shit sometimes that you've got to let slide every once in a while. But not completely.

"So are you saying that Mickey's lower class because she tried to slap the Black back into our friend turned Oreo?" I say, making everyone in the room shut up and listen. What did I say?

"You can't slap the Black back into someone, Jayd. And Nellie's just fine the way she is." How in the hell would he know how to get her back to her senses? As I watch Chance march off into the dressing room with Alia right behind him, I wonder what he meant by his comment about Mr. Weiner. What don't I know about the way these supposedly cool White men feel about us feisty Black girls? I intend to find out after school. It's time to get all our feelings out in the open.

~ 9 ~
Cleaning House

"Friends, how many of us have them?"

—BONE THUGS-N-HARMONY

I couldn't think about anything else for the last two periods of school except for Chance's comment about Jeremy's dad. I know his mom's a trip. But I never got that feeling from Mr. Weiner. Maybe it's because he's always drunk when I see him. But it wouldn't surprise me if he doesn't really care for Black women. Most folks around here have negative images in their heads when you say anything about a sistah's attitude. My mom says some of our own men don't like our fire either. But she also thinks they're the only ones who can handle us and appreciate our inner strength, something both Rah and KJ liked about me.

This whole thing's really got me thinking about my relationship with Jeremy. My mom warned me in my dream about friends versus frenemies. And, she wasn't just talking about my girls, I don't think. I feel like Jeremy's good to me and loves me, sort of. I think he likes the fire that makes me Jayd only when it complements him, and that ain't cool. If we're going to survive, that'll have to change. We need to get some things out in the open, and there's no time like the present to do that.

* * *

"Jeremy, does your dad have a problem with Black girls?" I ask as Jeremy and I walk hand in hand through the busy mall. We haven't been back since our embarrassing scene with KJ a few weeks ago. My gold *J* bangle sparkles as the sunlight beams through the glass ceiling, making me smile. I wish Mama would let me wear my jade bracelets every day. But she says they're precious and can be worn only on special occasions. I hope the Masquerade Ball is one of them. Besides being pretty, they're very powerful tools that help me focus my thoughts. And that'll be helpful if something does go down at the ball.

"What are you talking about?" Jeremy says, sipping on his extra-large cherry Icee as we wait for our Chinese food. South Bay Galleria has the best choice of restaurants in a mall I've ever seen.

"Chance said something about fueling Mr. Weiner's fire and others like him. What did he mean?" Jeremy, looking uncomfortable all of a sudden, has to take a bathroom break.

"I gotta take a leak before our food comes. Hold this for me," he says, leaving me standing in line and holding his frozen drink. As Jeremy enters the men's restroom to the right of the food court, I see Tania walk out of a maternity store across the way with her Yorkshire terrier—just like China's—peeking out of her Louis Vuitton bag. I would say it's the perfect time to question her about Jeremy, but this whole scene feels eerily familiar, and he'll be back any minute to finish our conversation. Noticing me, Tania heads my way. She's going to force me to confront her now anyway.

"Number three forty-six!" the lady behind the counter yells. The other customers look at their receipts, hoping it's their food. I know it's our order, but my hands are full and Jeremy's nowhere to be found. And I know Tania's not coming over here to help me.

"Jayd, so nice to see you outside of school. I hope Chance

is okay after today's unfortunate episode," Tania says with the fakest smile ever. She can teach Nellie all the ins and outs of being a perfect Oreo, even if she is Persian and not black. It may be a different mix, but the results are the same.

"Whatever, trick. What are you even doing here? Don't you have to finish planning Nellie's sabotage?" I say, tired of pretending with this girl. I have no patience for her worrisome ass right now. And where's her entourage? I'd think she'd have too many enemies to ever want to be seen alone in public. But maybe she's not comfortable sharing her pregnancy with everyone quite yet.

"Oh, Jayd, stop trying to be everyone's savior all the time and have some fun. Like me—I'm just getting some shopping done. Helps to alleviate stress," Tania says, fanning her hand like she's just had one of Mama's hot flashes. Nellie and this girl also have the diva aspect in common. "Um, I don't know if you know it or not," she says, rubbing her nonexistent belly with her left hand, also displaying her engagement ring and small shopping bag from Motherhood, "but I'm expecting." She's gleaming like she just hit the lotto.

"Congratulations," I say as sarcastically as possible. This girl's really a trip. My hands are turning numb from the cold drinks melting in my hand, just like they did in my dream.

"You sound as if you already knew," Tania says, a little disappointed, realizing it's not as devastating a blow as she'd planned, I guess. "Did Jeremy tell you? Did he also reveal that he's the father?" she adds, curious about how much I know. She seems apprehensive about something, but what exactly I can't put my finger on.

"Let's just say I had a little divine intuition," I respond, tired of her games.

"Oh. Well, since you know everything," she says, looking like she's going for the kill; she has the exact same look as she did in my dream, "tell him he and his family need to hurry up with the parental-rights paperwork. I know they don't want any little brown babies any more than my family wants any illegitimate ones running around. Smooches," she says, she and her little bitch in tow. What the hell just happened here?

"Hey, babe," Jeremy says, finally returning from the restroom. That must've been some piss. "Is the food up?" I forgot all about the damned food with Tania's little visit. I have a feeling she doesn't really want to give up the possibility of a family life with Jeremy. This is what some of these girls attend school for: to meet their husbands in the same circle as themselves. And she doesn't seem at all concerned about being pregnant and getting married her senior year. So it must be something with Jeremy and his family that's preventing her legitimate fairy tale from coming true.

"Yeah, it is. What's up with your family and brown babies?" I ask, getting straight to the heart of the matter as he slides our full tray from the cashier and looks around for an empty spot.

"Jayd, can we just eat without any questions?" he says, choosing a table on the other side of the large eating area next to the atrium. "Where's this coming from, anyway?" I follow him to our seats and get comfortable, ready for the showdown. I have to play him like chess, which is a lot like what Mama said to do—visualize my end result. And I want the truth as my checkmate.

"Well, I just got hit in a drive-by from your baby's mama," I say, taking the majority of soy-sauce packets from the tray and opening them. I love orange chicken and vegetable fried rice. It's one of my favorite meals, and I'm starving. I didn't get to eat at all today, and with all the excitement, I've worked up a ferocious appetite. "She said something about parental paperwork and no brown Weiner heirs," I say, stuffing a forkful of the steaming food into my mouth. This might explain why after years of marriage Jeremy's older brother and half-Black wife have no children. What's really going on here? Jeremy's slamming down his broccoli, chicken and steamed rice like it's his last meal. He missed lunch, too, and his appetite is at least twice the size of mine, I'm sure.

"Jayd, I really don't want to talk about this right now," he says without looking up. But I must persist. He can't keep me out in the dark on this one.

"Jeremy, look. This came to me, I didn't seek it out. So let me help if I can," I say, touching his hand from across the small table. He looks into my eyes, and without saying a word, I see all the pain he's trying to protect me from. He's hurting over this, and I can't help him because, for some reason, he thinks it's out of his hands.

"Look, Jayd, I don't want to fight. I just want to have dinner with my girl, catch a movie and chill," he says, sitting back in his chair, exhausted. In about five minutes Jeremy has managed to clean his plate and is now working on the package of egg rolls we're sharing, with the fortune cookies last on his list. Damn, he can throw down. Jeremy and Mickey should have an eating contest one day. But I somehow don't think that's ever going to happen.

"We can do all that and take care of business," I say while offering him a bite of my food. He accepts my fork and gives me a slight smile. "Let me in," I plead. "If you keep shutting me out, you're going to close the door for good, and I don't want that."

"Me neither. But some things, Jayd, you got to learn to let go. Tania and all her issues is one of those things," he says, rising to put his tray on the trash can next to our table while I quickly finish my plate. Our movie starts in twenty minutes, and I want to check out this Lucky Brand Jeans bag in Macy's before we go in. All the stores will be closed by the time the movie's over, and I need to price it so I can budget it into my next few checks, braiding money included. Sometimes a girl just needs to treat herself, and I've wanted an authentic bag for a while now. I'm tired of carrying this fake Coach around. Even if I can afford only the small satchel, I'm still getting my purse.

"Jeremy, both Chance and Tania alluded to some racial issues with your dad in the same day; that's no coincidence," I say, getting up to put my plate on top of the tray, which Jeremy takes and places into the automatic trash can. Those things still freak me out. "What aren't you telling me?"

"Look, Jayd, my parents have issues, okay?" Jeremy says, following me down the escalator toward Macy's. "I'm sure your family has things you don't necessarily want the world to know about." Well, he's got me there. But the difference is that if he asks me about my family drama, I'll tell him. So he should show me the same respect and trust.

"Okay, what kinds of issues?" Here we go, the truth-and-tell segment of the relationship. I hope he rises to the occasion. "And what does your dad have against Black girls?"

"Jayd, he doesn't have anything against Black girls. All his sons have Black women in their lives." Now that ain't really true. Christi and Tammy may be Black by blood but not in culture. I'm actually the first sistah any of them has ever brought home, and there's some obvious discomfort in that.

"That doesn't mean shit, Jeremy. That's like all the other bigots who say they can't be racist because they have Black friends. That line of reasoning doesn't fly." Momentarily distracted from our conversation, I see my purse sitting behind the glass case, just waiting for me. Too bad they don't have layaway here. I remember I asked this White saleslady about it when I first came to this mall last year. She looked at me like I was speaking Mandarin.

"May I help you, miss?" a saleslady, who reminds me of

Mama, says from behind the counter. Jeremy's standing behind me, watching me envy the expensive bag.

"Yes, how much for this leather satchel?" I ask. I wonder what it's like to never have to ask about price and just pick out what you want. I wouldn't know about that lifestyle, but I assume that's the way Tania and Jeremy have lived all their lives.

"Two hundred and twenty-eight dollars," she says, like she just told me the price for a piece of gum. Well, I guess I won't be getting that bag until my birthday because that's how long it's going to take me to save up that kind of money.

"Thank you," I say, turning around to walk out of the store toward the theater. We have about ten more minutes before the movie starts, and even after that slamming meal, we're still going to need candy, popcorn and drinks.

"Wait a minute. You're not going to try it on?" Jeremy says. I think he likes to watch me model things for him. He rarely lets me eye anything without actually touching it.

"Jeremy, it's on my wish list. Besides, we have a movie to catch and a conversation to finish," I say, pulling him out of the quiet department store and back into the buzzing mall. It's Friday night, and it's packed in here. The nail shop has a line out the door, the stores are overcrowded and the movie theater is no different.

"What conversation? I thought we were finished," he says, wishing that were true. He has to know me better than that by now.

"Not until you answer my questions," I persist as we stand in line for our tickets. I love going out with Jeremy not only because he always pays for everything but because he's such a gentleman about it. He never even mentions money on a date, when we're at lunch or if we're just kicking it after school. He always has my back when it comes to that.

"Jayd, my dad has issues with loud, rude people in general. It's not just Black girls," he says, cutting to the chase. "Chance said that because Mickey's a prime example of what it means to lose control, and she just happens to be black." Now we're getting somewhere.

"So are you saying if it was a White girl who went off like Mickey did today, your dad would have a problem with her, too?" Before answering, Jeremy looks confused, like the thought never occurred to him before.

"Yeah, I guess so. But I've never seen a White girl do what Mickey did today," he says. And I guess in his reality that's true. But that's a problem with me. He has a definite idea in his mind of what Black women are like compared to White women, and that has to change.

"So your dad doesn't want any brown babies because he thinks they'll be loud?" I ask, trying to get the rest of the truth out of him. I know there's more to this story than what he's telling me.

"No, Tania's a completely separate issue," Jeremy says, purchasing the tickets from the automatic machine and opening the double doors. "She wants to get married, and I sure as hell don't. That's the end of that." But, that ain't what Tania said, and I don't think she just threw in the little brown bay-bay kid for the hell of it.

"Jeremy, why don't your older brother and his wife have any babies?" I ask. Jeremy gets a sullen look across his face, like I've just sparked up a very painful topic.

"She lost a baby in high school and couldn't have any children after that," he says, not going any further. I wonder if it had anything to do with the car accident Reid's family caused?

"I'm sorry," I say. I'm not going to push the subject any more right now. But I still feel like he's hiding something.

"Jayd, would you mind finding us a seat? I'm going to get our snacks. Red Vines and bottled water, right?" he says, knowing exactly what I want. He's going to have his usual popcorn and Milk Duds, I assume. Maybe I should stop interrogating him and have some fun. I need to push the bull of the week out of my head, and chilling with my man and watching *How She Move* are the perfect distractions. I'm not completely comfortable with the way our conversation ended, but I'll settle with the progress we've made so far. It's just like Mama says: you have to start cleaning the entire house one room at a time.

The opening credits are rolling, and I'm ready to completely zone out into the dance movie, but Jeremy's not back from the concession stand yet. I love to watch people step. It's been over ten minutes, and the lines move pretty quickly here. I wonder what the holdup is.

"Hey, babe," Jeremy says, passing the boxes of candy and popcorn to me. He takes the two bottles of water out of his jean pockets and places them in the cup holders adjacent to the chairs.

"I thought you got lost," I say, moving my sweater out of his seat so he can sit down. I know he needs to stretch his long legs, so I always make it a point to pick a row with an empty aisle seat.

"No, I just had to take care of something real quick," he says, placing a Macy's bag in my lap. Oh, no, he didn't.

"Jeremy, what did you do?" I ask, opening the pretty gift to reveal my soft brown bag.

"You shouldn't have to wait for this," he says, pulling it out and setting the empty shopping bag on the floor as the movie begins.

"Thank you," I say, gently kissing him on the lips. Although I'm happy about my gift, there's still something wrong with this picture. He can be caring enough to buy me an expensive purse but not to tell me the whole truth about his family? Is he trying to buy my silence or just appease me so I'll forget about the other stuff? Either way, it doesn't make me feel good to have my emotions equated with a material object. And besides, I wanted to buy the purse myself. There's no substitute for my self-worth.

~ 10 ~
Like Water for Chocolate

"I'm the blues in your left thigh/
Trying to become the funk in your right."

—LORENZ TATE/LOVE JONES SOUNDTRACK

After Friday night's date, I didn't feel like talking to Jeremy about why he bought me my purse. If I said he just got it because he thought it would substitute for telling me the whole truth, he might be offended, and I don't feel like going there with him. Jeremy shuts down when his feelings get hurt, like most men I know. And yesterday was so busy at work, I went right to sleep when I got home. Rah called and invited me to the session last night, but that wasn't on my agenda. I just wanted to chill.

For the first time in a long time I called in sick to work this morning. Summer was disappointed but sounded really concerned. I started my cycle yesterday at work, and she gave me this book by a sister named Queen Afua with all kinds of recipes for healing a woman's body. Thank goodness Simply Wholesome is like a modern botanica, with all kinds of herbal teas and tinctures to help ease my discomfort. I need to take a break from all those bougie-ass people while I'm on my cycle. I already agreed to braid Rah's hair later this afternoon before going back to Mama's, and that'll make up for the day's pay I'm missing. It's only noon, and I'm sure he's still asleep.

"Jayd, you need to put a heating pad in your stomach and elevate your feet. You know better than to lie there all scrunched up in a ball, waiting for that Tylenol to kick in. Be proactive," my mom says, bouncing around the living room, all excited. She's got a tennis date with her new friend Karl, and she's on cloud nine. I like this guy though, from what I've heard about him. Today will be the first time we actually meet. My mom looks stunning in her purple Serena tennis dress. She bought it yesterday, along with a pair of new kicks. Nike must love her credit-card company right about now.

"Coming!" she says, responding to the knock at the door. She closes the hall closet door and walks over to me, touching my stomach. He's punctual; I like that.

"I'll be back around five to take you home," she says, plugging the heating pad into the wall next to the small sofa. Home's relative. I feel more at home when I'm here because I can chill and be myself. But without Mama and the spirit room, I feel like anywhere else I stay can be only temporary, no matter how convenient my mom's house may be.

"Hi, Karl," my mom says, flashing her brilliant jade eyes and bright smile as she opens the door, captivating her new man. He's not so bad-looking himself. Karl's tall, brown and athletic, just like she likes them. Dating Ras Joe was a bit out of the norm for Lynn Marie. But he had money and spoiled her, which is right in alignment with her true desires. "This is my daughter, Jayd," she says, taking her jacket and tennis bag off the coatrack.

"You look nice, Lynn. Well, hello, there, young lady," Karl says, waving from the hall. My mom doesn't let dudes in on the first date. She has many rules in her game.

"Hello," I say, almost grunting. I feel like I could pass out from my pain at any moment. The heating pad's warming up and somewhat soothes my discomfort. "Be careful with her," I add, teasing the preppy pair.

"Get some rest, baby, and I'll see you in a little while," my mom says, closing the door behind her. I need some peanut

M&M's or something, and I've already devoured all the chocolate in this house. *"Here's my ghetto story,"* Rah's new ring tone sings. The song put me in such a good mood after hearing him play it the other day, I figured he'd reclaimed the right of having a signature tune of his own.

"What's up?" I grunt. I hope I feel better by the time he gets here.

"Hey, girl. You sound like shit. What's wrong?" he asks. "I know you ain't trying to get out of braiding a brotha's hair, are you?"

"No," I say. "I actually need the money since I missed work today."

"You missed work? This must be serious," Rah says, going into full daddy mode. Whenever I would get sick back in the day, he'd take the day off with me. Since Mama loves him, she'd always let Rah stay.

"Oh, just the same monthly visitor I've had for the past six years and counting, I pray." Mama's always quick to remind us of the blessing of fertility and to never take it for granted, no matter how uncomfortable it may sometimes get being a woman. It's hard to remain grateful when I want to pass out from the excruciating cramps.

"Oh, I see," he says, sounding sympathetic. If any dude could feel my pain, it would be him. "You want me to bring you a Snickers when I come over?" Rah offers, instinctively knowing it's what I crave most, even when I'm not on my period. How could someone so seemingly perfect for me also be my worst heartbreak ever?

"Yeah, that sounds good. What time will you be here?" I shift the heating pad from the front of my body to my back, which is also sore. The last thing I feel like doing is sitting up braiding. But for Rah, I'll bear it.

"I'll be there soon. But you don't have to get up if you don't want to. I'm in no rush," he says.

"Good, because right now the only thing I can do is lie here." All I've done this morning is make two phone calls—one to my job and the other to my boyfriend. I talked to Jeremy a while ago, and he said he and his brothers are all spending the day together. Well, Rah is like my brother—with benefits—so I guess I'm having a brother day, too.

"No problem. I'll see you in a few," he says, hanging up the phone. To tell the truth, I'm almost looking forward to seeing the candy bar more than Rah.

When Rah arrives, I get up to let him in and instantly return to my warm spot on the couch. The meds have finally kicked in, and I was just starting to get comfortable.

"How are you feeling?" he says, closing the door behind him before sitting on the small space I've left for him at the end of the sofa. "Here's your fix." He passes me the small brown paper bag with my goodies in it.

"Kingsize," I say. "You spoil me." And it's true. Rah has always paid attention to my likes and dislikes. We don't have money to buy all the fancy stuff Jeremy can afford, but that never seems to matter. He always makes sure that anything I want I get.

"Yeah, the right way," he says, noticing my new purse on the coffee table. "Another guilt gift?" He points to the bag. I haven't used it yet because I just can't bring myself to. I really wanted to buy the purse myself. Jeremy took all the joy out of it for me. But it's still a fly bag.

"Don't start," I groan as he looks back at me, arching his eyebrows with a smirk on his face. Rah's giving me his *you know I'm right* look. I can't stand it when he does that.

"Jayd, how long you gone stay with this fool?" he says, watching me tear open my Snickers and devour it in three bites. That hit the spot. I'm glad Rah doesn't mind watching me eat. I've got to be able to throw down around whoever I'm with.

"As long as I can," I say. Who knows how long that'll be,

but I'm not going to allow him to cut it short. I'm letting nature run its course, even if it is a rough road.

"He's not even taking you to the Halloween ball, is he?" Why does he know so much about my school's business?

"How do you even know that?" I say, chewing my last mouthful of chocolate.

"Gossip travels up the 405. You didn't know?" he says, making me giggle. He can be so silly sometimes. "Nah, but for real, though, girl, you deserve better. I'd rather you still be with that punk-ass nigga KJ than the White boy, shawty." Rah sounds real sincere about his concern for me, but he should've been more concerned when he was the one hurting me.

"Don't worry about me; I can take care of myself," I say, turning off my heating pad and rising from the couch. I feel much better and energetic after my chocolate rush. Now I can braid some hair.

"I don't doubt that," he says, taking his bottled water out of his paper bag. "But I think you make bad decisions when it comes to dudes."

"Now ain't that the pot calling the kettle black!" I yell from the bathroom. I need to get a bag for all my hair supplies when I braid: aloe-vera gel, tea-tree oil, Mama's coconut oil, several combs and clips and rubber bands, a mirror and some leave-in conditioner. All this for some cornrows. But that's what makes them so hot when I'm the one braiding.

"Well, I'm actually calling the kettle white," he says, laughing at his own witty comeback. "Ouch!" he yells as the comb I flung across the room hits him in the head. "You and Mickey need anger-management classes."

"Shut the hell up," I say, straddling the couch behind him as Rah slides down to sit on the floor. I place all my hair goods next to me on the couch, ready to get started.

"Tell me I'm lying." The truth is, I can't. It's another Williams Women trait I have to deal with: our taste in men.

"Whatever, Rah. All I'm saying is it ain't your business no more, and if you want to stay friends you're going to have to start respecting my relationship with Jeremy, which also means no more sneak kisses," I say, playfully smacking him in the head with my comb.

"You know you liked it," he says, closing his eyes as I begin to massage his scalp. I like to condition his hair before I begin combing through the shiny black mane. His thick Afro is so soft it doesn't need much oil to make it pliable when I braid.

"That's not the point. Don't mess this up for me, Rah. You've already got a girl, and we've been down this road before," I say, doubting my own sincerity. I wish I could honestly say I didn't want to be with Rah. Ever since Nigel and Rah came back into my life, it's felt like old times when the three of us—plus whatever girl Nigel was with back then—hung tight. It felt good, safe and secure.

"Yeah, we have, so let's see what's on television; I'm tired of talking about your denial issues," he says, picking up the remote and knocking over my bag.

"My bad," Rah says, setting the bag upright. "Are you thirsty?" He hands me the bottle of water sitting next to my purse.

"I actually want another Snickers," I say, accepting the cold drink. I know that seems greedy, but I'm just being true to my feelings, kinda like I'm doing with Rah and Jeremy; I can't help but love them both. It's only natural, especially after all Rah and I've been through. But it shouldn't have anything to do with my relationship with Jeremy. I hope they both understand their unique roles in my life and don't cross each other's paths again. But knowing Rah, it's only a matter of time before he officially begins his sabotage mission.

"Girl, you better quit. All that sugar ain't good for you," he says as he molds his neck into my thighs while I begin to

sculpt his scalp. Parting Rah's hair is so relaxing and powerful to me. I don't know why, but knowing that I put his hair
in braids gives me a link with him no other girl has. My cornrows are signature. Jeremy should let me braid his hair.
Maybe we can establish a similar bond.

"I know. But like all things sinful, not being good for me
doesn't stop me from wanting it," I say, making myself heat
up. Rah's energy is so overwhelming, especially having him
this close to me. I'm getting the same feeling I got at homecoming when we were walking around South Bay's campus
at night. Why can't I shake this fool's power over me?

"Is that right, Miss Jackson?" Rah says, amused by my response. He turns the cable channel to Showtime, where *Hus-
tle & Flow*, one of my favorite movies, is on. I think most
people misunderstand what this film's about. When I saw the
advertisements, all they talked about was a Black pimp in the
South and his White ho, and that isn't what this story's about
at all.

"You remember when we went to see this?" he says, reminding me of one of our last dates as a couple. I saw it only
because Rah insisted, and I'm glad he did. "I still have this
soundtrack in my rotation."

"Yeah, that shit's hot," I say. As I become entranced in the
neat parts and shiny braids I'm weaving into his head, my favorite part comes on. The kiss between Djay and Shug em-
bodies the true essence of the movie for me; it's all about
Black love.

"Damn, girl, that's why we got suspended," he says, making me recall our first kiss behind our math class at Family
Christian. We got busted by my evil seventh-grade math
teacher and were put on probation for "passionate kissing"
the remainder of the school year. As embarrassed as I was, I
didn't care if we got caught again. I just wanted to keep kiss-

ing him. Rah was the first and by far the best kisser I've ever had. Aw, hell, this isn't good. He needs to turn the channel, and now.

"Rah, see what else is on. We don't need to be watching this and going down memory lane," I say, attempting to snatch the remote from his control.

"You need to concentrate on my hair and let me handle the entertainment," he says, pushing my hands back. "What's wrong? Good memories giving you hot flashes?" He's alluding to the secret only he and I share. I haven't told any of my other friends about my powers and their effects on me. Nigel and Misty have an idea about Mama's reputation in the hood but not about our complete lineage. Rah's the only friend I can trust with my true self.

"Shut up," I say, again smacking him in the head before I continue braiding. My mom will be home in a few hours, and I want to make sure I take my time with his hair and get packed up before she gets back. She doesn't like me moving slow on Sundays or any other day she has to take me back to Compton. My mom stays there long enough to holler at my grandparents, Bryan and Jay, and then she's out. Lynn Mae's not one for staying on the east side any longer than necessary.

"What time's your mom getting back?" he asks, knowing my routine. It must be nice to have a single home, no matter how dysfunctional it may be.

"About five," I say.

"Cool," he says, pulling out a blunt and lighting it, in full chill mode. My mom smokes sometimes, too, so she won't notice the lingering scent after we burn some incense and air the joint out. I'm glad Rah doesn't pressure me to smoke. He knows it's not my thing. I'm going to miss this freedom once I return to Mama's. But I am looking forward to getting this week over. It's going to be busy at home with Mama's Halloween clients becoming more demanding as the unholy day approaches, and I want to get the Masquerade Ball over, too. I better enjoy my last few hours of chill time before the storm begins.

I walk into the gymnasium turned cemetery, my Afro wig in full effect as I strut across the floor in my high-heeled boots. I look around and can barely make out the bodies, due to the false fog generating through the large room, but I can feel Rah's presence and taste his chocolate-coated kisses on my lips. I feel like I need a drink of cool water to quench my parched throat, so I begin looking for the refreshment table on the other side of the gym.

There are spiderwebs and bloody mannequins hanging from the ceiling, which further obstruct my vision as I make my way through the crowd. In the center of the basketball court are three huge bubbling cauldrons where people are lined up to take their turns bobbing for apples; Tania, Nellie and Laura are in the middle row. I notice that Tania, who's naturally in front of her followers, has an apple hidden up her sleeve. When her turn comes, she refuses to put her blindfold on and bobs for her fruit with perfect aim. She then slips her hidden apple in the water, and Nellie follows her lead, just as Tania expected.

"Go for that one, Nellie," Tania says, pointing to the planted target with a wicked grin. Her demeanor fits her costume perfectly: a sluttish witch. I feel like I'm in a twisted version of Snow White *and I need to save Nellie from the jealous stepmother's poisonous plan, but I'm too late. By the time I run over to where they are, she's already bitten into the tainted fruit infected with worms, which quickly spread all over Nellie's face, freaking out her and everyone else around.*

Remember, Jayd, true friends help each other in their time of need, even when they won't admit they need it, *my mom says, her thoughts again invading my space.*

"Jayd, get up," Bryan says, reminding me it's Monday morning and I need to wake up. The buses around here wait for no one, no matter how cute I may be. Damn, I knew something was going to go down at the ball. I've got to get through to Nellie before Saturday or she may never recover from this one. There's no limit to Tania's evil, and I intend to expose her for the vixen she truly is.

~ 11 ~
Yuck Mouth

*"Smile for me, Daddy/
Let me see your grill."*

—NELLIE

After my dream last night about Nellie's unfortunate snack, I felt a little nauseated this morning and made some raspberry tea for breakfast. My monthly visitor should be gone by Wednesday, but until then Mama's herbal capsules will help me deal with the inconvenience. No drugs they sell in the store will ever beat Mama's herbs.

The bus rides to school this morning were unusually annoying, with my cramps still in full effect. It's break, and I really just want to lie down on a bench and soak up some of the sun's warmth; it always relaxes me. I just need to switch off my books before I chill. But to my surprise, Nellie's waiting at my locker. This can't be good.

"Hey, Jayd," Nellie says, acting like we've been cool for the past few weeks. Something must've happened over the weekend to make this broad come up to me and chat. Maybe she had the same dream last night. If so, I can't blame her for looking for help.

"Nellie," I say, giving her the cold shoulder. I really don't want to make this easy for her. She needs to learn that real friends are not disposable, and I'm going to be just the one to teach her that lesson.

"I know I've been kind of unavailable lately," she says,

twisting her straightened hair around her finger like a five-year-old who's been caught wearing her mama's favorite shoes. "But I just wanted to see if we could catch up."

"Now?" I say, looking at the clock on the wall by the main entrance. There are only ten minutes left until third period, and I really want to grab a quick snack and chill out by myself. Jeremy didn't have too much to say to me on the short ride from the bus stop this morning, so if I'm going to talk with anyone, it would be him. I'm in no mood for an intense conversation with Nellie right now.

"Yes, if you have time," Nellie says. I take my books out of my backpack and place the ones I don't need back into my locker before closing it shut. "I really just want to see how you and Mickey are doing," she adds nervously. What's really going on with her? I don't feel like this is an innocent mission to rekindle our friendship.

"What's really up with you, Nellie?" I say, speed walking down the busy corridor toward the back exit. I can see that the line for the nutrition stand across the way is still long. Damn. I need to get something in my stomach before class. Mrs. Peterson never lets us finish our food in her room, and I can't afford to be late. "I don't have much time before the bell rings, so spit it out," I say, taking my place in line behind the other hungry students.

"Has Mickey said anything to you about me?" she asks, again with the nervous twitch.

"Anything like what?" I ask. Oh, hell, no, Nellie didn't start some more shit with Mickey. "After barely missing getting knocked out the other day, I'd think you would leave her be." I move one more spot closer to the front.

"That was totally uncalled for," Nellie says, tossing her hair over her shoulders and looking down at everyone around us, even if she's shorter than them. "She can be so ghetto, don't you agree?" This girl is worse than ever before, and I'm starting to lose any interest I have in helping her. Maybe it's just the hormones talking, but I kinda wish Mickey would come over here now and finish what she started the other day. This time Chance won't be here to save her.

"Did you at least apologize to Chance?" I say. He's still a little pissed at me, but I'm sure it'll pass. Chance really means well and has a sweet heart. Besides, I need all the true friends I can find, even if their weaknesses work my nerves sometimes.

"Yes, I did, and he forgave me." Nellie grins. I don't like this feeling I'm getting from her. She's hiding something, and if it has to do with Mickey, I won't be able to save her this time. I might even have to jump in on Mickey's side, depending on what it is. "But if Mickey mentions anything about me, will you please let me know?" she says, forgetting that we're no longer friends.

"I don't have any loyalty toward you anymore, Nellie," I say, almost reaching my goal. The popcorn behind the counter smells so good I think I'll take a small bag. It'll be easy to down while walking to government. "Or have you forgotten the ice chips falling from your shoulder?"

"Look, Jayd, that's just a part of the job," she says, again taking her crown too seriously.

"Nellie, give it up!" I yell. "You don't have a job. As a matter of fact, you've never worked a day in your princess-ass life. Now, I've had it with you and your sometimey ass. Whatever you did to Mickey, you're on your own. I can't believe you'd use me like this." I'm more pissed and hungry than ever.

"I know a little something about Jeremy and Tania, if you're interested," she says, diverting my attention away from the lady behind the counter who's now ready to take my order. I must admit, I'm curious to know who the devil told Nellie. But gossip ain't my style. If I'm going to find out anything, it'll have to be straight from the source.

"Excuse me, miss," the lady says, irritated that we're holding up the line. "What'll it be?"

"A small popcorn, please," I say, ignoring Nellie and pulling out my petite purse from the side of my backpack. I still haven't used my new bag, and I don't know that I ever will. "Thank you." I take the warm treat and walk toward my third period, Nellie still hot on my trail.

"Jayd, I think you'll want to hear what I have to say," she says, making a desperate attempt to engage me in her madness.

"Nellie, I don't read about nor do I want to be a *Gossip Girl*," I say, alluding to her favorite books. I never did get into them, but now I can see why Nellie's so intrigued.

"Fine, suit yourself," she says angrily. "But you'll be sorry when you do get wind of the truth." She stops in front of the Main Hall as I pass it by and continue walking toward my class. The warning bell should be ringing any minute, and students are starting to wrap up their conversations and make-out sessions.

"I have a feeling you'll be sorrier than I will when Mickey finds out whatever it is you're hiding," I say as I look back at her. Whatever she did must be really bad because my last comment just made her flawless dark skin turn gray. What the hell did she do, and what does she know about Jeremy and Tania that I need to know? I guess I'll just have to wait and see like everyone else.

"What's up for lunch?" Jeremy says as we walk toward his car, with Chance and Matt not far behind. "Mexican or Italian? Lady's choice." That popcorn didn't do anything but tease me at break, and I've been waiting for the last two hours to get to this point.

"A chimichanga sounds really good right now." I can actually make chimichangas pretty well. Maggie gave me the

recipe last year after she brought some to school for our an-
nual cultural festival in March. I've been sprung on them
ever since.

"Mexican it is," he says, swooping out of the parking lot
toward the beach. I know he wishes he was surfing right
now, because even I want to dip my body in the sapphire
waves. The gentle breeze cools my face from the hot classroom I just came out of. My math class smells like a dirty
shoe, and I feel like I'm still inside it.

Chance and Matt are right behind us, bumping Mims's
"This is Why I'm Hot." I love the remix. Jeremy turns his
music up and drowns out Chance's car.

"Hey, I'm listening to that," I say, reaching for the dial and
turning down the Smiths. I love *Charmed* just as much as the
next person, but there's a difference between hearing the
song on television and bumping it in the car. As I get back
into my groove, Jeremy turns his radio back up, again interrupting my vibe.

"The driver gets to pick the music, remember?" He smiles,
but I'm not amused. I know he likes some hip-hop, but his
true love is alternative. And that makes for a strenuous ride
sometimes. I like to bump down the block, like when Rah,
Nigel or Mickey and I roll. Alternative just don't get me in
that chill mood all the time.

"I know, baby, but can we just finish listening to this song?
It's almost over," I say, trying to sweet-talk my man. There's a
lot of give-and-take in this relationship, mostly from me, it
seems.

"Jayd, why would you rather listen to Chance's radio six
feet back than to mine right here? Our sound systems are
similar." Yeah, but the tunes are different.

"Never mind," I say, giving in. I just want to eat and chill
out for a minute before going back to school. It's been a long
Monday, and I'm ready to go home and call it a day.

"You want to go in?" he asks, pulling up to Alonzo's, the best fast-food Mexican restaurant in the South Bay.

"Drive-through," I say, shifting my weight in the leather seats. As Jeremy orders our food, I feel a little wet and notice a spot has surfaced on my gray sweats. I'll be damned if I didn't bleed through my pad. What the hell? Thank goodness I have a sweater in my backpack to wrap around my waist. But I can't guarantee it will save me for the rest of the day. I'm going to have to call Mama to get a pass home. When it comes to my cycle, Mama never questions me wanting to be in my own bed. I simultaneously grab my phone and sweater from my bag as Jeremy places our order.

"Hello?" Mama says, sounding like she's been interrupted. *All My Children's* on, so I know she's not in the mood to talk.

"Mama, it's me. I need to come home," I say, trying to be as discreet as possible. I'm not comfortable enough to tell Jeremy about this. It'll be like farting in front of him, and we're just not there yet.

"Haven't I told you to carry an extra set of clothes when you're on your cycle?" she says, instinctively knowing why I'm calling. "I'll call the office and get your uncle Bryan to come and pick you up. He just got in from Miracle Market, so I'll send him on over there."

"Thank you," I say, hanging up my cell and reaching for my backpack. I'm glad to have the rest of the day off. And with tomorrow being a short day for teacher meetings, the end of the week will come quickly. But I'm sure there'll be enough drama throughout for it to seem as long as it usually is.

"Here you go, Jayd," Jeremy says, handing me the cold drinks before reaching for the hot food. I can't wait to get started on my fried burrito.

"Thank you," I say, pulling a tortilla chip out of the bag while we pull up and wait for our friends. When we get back to campus I'll go straight to the attendance office, get my pass and wait outside for Bryan. Knowing him, he'll probably demand I give him gas money or something. I don't blame him; his old Chevy van uses up a grip of gas, and Redondo Beach ain't around the corner from home.

When we get back to campus, Mickey and Nigel are in his car kicking it. We pull up right beside them, but they hardly notice. I'm almost finished with my food, and my Coca-Cola is next on the list. I can take my time since I'll be waiting for another half hour, at least. But everyone else has to get back to class. Speaking of which, KJ, Del and C Money pull up on the other side of Nigel, creating an awkward sandwich. Everyone exits their cars almost at the same time as the warning bell rings.

"What up, Jayd?" KJ says, showing off his new grill. I notice that his homies each have one of their own. Oh, no, they didn't waste their money on some foul shit like that.

"What the hell is that in your mouth?" I say, closing the car door. Jeremy and Chance are getting a kick out of me roasting KJ. Why is it different now than when it's about Tania?

"What do you think it is?" KJ slurs, being a smart-ass.

"The girls love it, Jayd, ain't that right, Mickey?" Del says, making her laugh. She and Del have known each other since elementary school and have been homies ever since.

"I think they make your breath stink," Mickey says, following Nigel out of his Impala and up the steps leading into the main office.

"Girl, you don't know what you're talking about," C Money says as he exits the backseat of KJ's hooopty. "Girl's love it when Daddy smiles the bling at them." C Money can be such an ass sometimes.

"Whatever. All I know is that it looks cheap and Mickey's right—it does make your breath stink," I say as Jeremy grabs my backpack and wraps his free arm around my waist while I finish the last of my lunch. KJ and his crew walk up the side steps and through the front gate, entering the main quad. Chance and Matt are still in his car having a smoke before heading down to drama class, and Jeremy and I lean up against the steps. Jeremy's hand moves down my back, making me feel self-conscious.

"Not too low, baby," I say, feeling my sweater begin to slip down my waist. I'm going to have to toss the rest of my drink so I can hold on to my little secret until I get home. All I need is for KJ and his crew to see me blemished; I'll have a new nickname all around campus before Bryan gets here.

"Why? What you hiding back there?" he says, tickling me and not understanding that this isn't the time to play. I glide his hand back up to my waist while giving him a look that stops him once and for all.

"Jayd, you want to go to the mall after school?" Mickey says from the top of the steps ahead of us. Thank God for the interruption.

"Nah, I'm actually going home early," I say, breaking the news to everyone around. "What about tomorrow? It's an early day."

"Oh, that's right," Mickey says with a sly smile. If it weren't for football practice and mandatory weight days when we have short days, I'm sure she and Nigel would have other plans. "All right then, Jayd. Are you feeling okay?"

"Yeah, I'm cool. I just had a doctor's appointment I forgot about, that's all," I lie, silencing Jeremy and Mickey without any more questions. Jeremy doesn't look like he believes me but doesn't push any further. "Y'all better go before the bell rings," I say, dumping my trash into the bin outside the office door.

"All right, baby. I'll call you after school," Jeremy says, kissing me on the lips before heading through the double doors,

right behind Chance, who nods me good-bye. When I finally
enter the double doors and make a right toward the attendance office, I can see Nellie up ahead talking to Misty. Noticing my approach, they both head out in opposite directions.
What the hell do they have to talk about?

I feel something very bad stirring in the wind. All this gos-
siping is going a bit too far. Maybe my dream about Nellie's
rotten mouth was alluding to her spreading shit around
about Mickey. I know KJ and his boys are the ones with grills,
but it looks like Nellie's the real yuck mouth around here.
Whatever mess she's gotten herself into with Misty, I hope
she's ready for the repercussions, because knowing Mickey,
payback will definitely be a bad bitch.

~ 12 ~
The Cuss-Out

"I said you hold back and if you ain't heard /
But them are fighting words."

—MACY GRAY

When I got home yesterday from school, I changed my clothes, took a shower and went straight to bed and stayed there until this morning. I had to spend my break and lunch today making up my homework from last night. Luckily I was able to get my English homework done in Spanish class; my first period's always boring. I'm actually looking forward to kicking it at the mall with Mickey, if for no other reason than to see if I can exchange this bag Jeremy got for me. I've been hiding it in my locker all day and still don't know what to do.

"Jayd, are you ready?" Mickey says as I close my locker and head toward the end of the barren hall. Mickey usually parks in the back parking lot; her pink Regal is too special to be with all the popular kids' cars.

"Yes, I am," I say as Alicia Keys announces Rah's call. "What up, man?" I say, happy to hear from him. We texted each other yesterday, but I haven't talked to him since Sunday.

"Nothing, shawty. What are you up to?" he asks.

"Well, right now I'm about to get into Mickey's car and ride up to the mall. And you," I say, knowing his school's on the same schedule as mine, like all the other schools in our district.

"I was about to head up to your school and work out with my boy. You leaving right now?" he says, sounding as cute as ever. It wouldn't be a good idea for Mickey and I to be in the weight room. That's how rumors get started, and we already have enough of that going around as it is.

"Yes. You know I have things to do, people to see," I tease. Jeremy's surfing with his crew, so it's just me and my girl this afternoon.

"Whatever, man. Sounds like you're avoiding me," Rah says, trying to make me feel guilty. But it isn't going to work. I don't like his pressuring me about my Jeremy right now. "Or have you finally come to your senses and decided to take that bribe bag back?" How does he read my mind like that?

"You know what, Rah?" I say, trying to divert his radar; I have enough people in my head already. "You think too much. I'll holla back," I say, sitting down in the hot car as Mickey turns on the engine, the speakers immediately bumping E-40's bass line, putting me in a good mood.

"You do that. Peace, queen," he says, sounding like he's from the east coast. His dad's originally from New York, and even though he's on lockdown in Atlanta, they still talk often, sharing knowledge however they can. I know Rah and Kamal miss their dad, especially with a crazy mama like theirs at home. And the South ain't nothing nice, especially not when a brotha's got three strikes, so I know it has to be hard for him, too.

"Peace, Rah," I say before folding my phone shut. I reach into my backpack and retrieve my dilapidated fake Coach bag, slipping the cell back inside.

"Girl, you need a new purse," Mickey says as she pulls out of the overpacked parking lot heading toward the Galleria with the majority of the crowd. Whoever's not going to the beach is definitely going to the mall. "I think Macy's is having a sale. I have some coupons in my purse." I take out my leather Lucky satchel and hold it, showing her my guilt gift.

"I already have one," I say, sounding sad. I really want this bag, but it's the principle of it all that's killing it for me. Jeremy and I still haven't finished our discussion about his racist daddy, and I need some answers. I feel like if I wear this bag, I can't continue to grill him about that or Tania, and that isn't worth it to me.

"Damn, girl, you hit the jackpot," she says, almost hitting the car in front of us as she grabs the fly bag off my lap. "Why you ain't wearing it?"

"Because it's hush money," I say, finally speaking the words out loud. Rah's right; I can't keep this bag. But I hate to let it go.

"What the hell are you talking about, Jayd?" Mickey says, turning down the music so she can hear me better. All the White folks gawk at us as we cruise down Artesia while playing our loud-ass sounds. I know they're thinking *What are those ghetto girls doing here?* And Mickey's gangstered-out Compton bumper sticker doesn't help them to think otherwise, which is just fine with me. We already look out of place with all the Audis and Land Cruisers driving by. But like Daddy says, classic cars are made to last, and so is Black culture. It's one of his favorite sermons to preach when Bryan starts to complain about wanting a new car.

"The only reason Jeremy bought me this purse was to keep me from asking him about Tania and his daddy," I say, clutching the bag close as we circle the parking lot, looking for a spot close to the door. Mickey likes to be close to all exits wherever she goes; according to her, you never know when you'll have to make a run for it.

"Jayd, you get too caught up in the whys and hows of shit," she says, expertly parking the car and turning off the engine. "You need to sport that bag like a trophy that you earned for putting up with that White boy and his bull." She grabs her large Dooney & Bourke bag before getting out. Her man leaves her wanting for nothing. Well, all except for Nigel apparently, because she can't get enough of him. I sure do hope she's using protection, not that it'll save her from the beating her man will give her if he finds out about Nigel.

"I can't do that. Besides, I wanted to buy the bag myself," I say, grabbing both my new bag and old purse before joining Mickey on the other side of the car. "He took all the fun out of me having it."

"Girl, you need to reevaluate the way you deal with dudes," she says, leading the way into the crowded mall. The smell of various perfumes overwhelms my nose, making me sneeze.

"Bless you," says the saleslady behind the counter.

"Thank you," I say, walking past her counter and toward the shoe and purse section. I love the smell of new leather.

"Jayd, are you seriously going to take back that two-hundred-dollar bag your rich boyfriend bought so you can spend your own hard-earned money on it? That makes absolutely no sense to me." Well, when Mickey puts it like that, it does sound kind of stupid. But I've got to do it, no matter how it makes me look.

"Mickey, I'd feel terrible if I kept this bag, and that's that," I say, approaching the counter with my bag in its original wrapping, stuffing included. I didn't bring the shopping bag, because it wouldn't fit in my backpack, and I didn't want to risk getting it dirty on the bus.

"May I help you?" the snooty White lady says from her register without looking up.

"Yes, I'd like to return this bag," I say, placing the brown beauty on the counter. I am going to miss her. But the next time we're together, it'll be for the right reasons and feel much better. The lady looks at the bag, then up at me, then at Mickey. I know she thinks we stole it; it's written all over her face.

"Do you have a receipt?" she asks, anticipating a negative response.

"Uh, no. It was a gift," I say, feeling nervous. This trick looks like she's caught Bonnie and Clyde red-handed. Damn, not this shit again. Mickey's looking around for the exits, and I'm right with her.

"And you didn't receive a gift receipt or a shopping bag at the very least?" she says, inspecting the immaculate purse with a twisted look on her face. If I were White or looked like I had money, my not having a receipt wouldn't be an issue, I'm sure.

"Look, lady," Mickey says, pissed at this broad's attitude. "She just wants to return the damned bag. The price tag's on it, and it hasn't been worn, so what's the problem?" Mickey's antagonizing the already irritated saleswoman, who has now called her manager over to help deal with us.

"The problem is," the manager says, an older White man who looks like the pimp of the place, "we don't accept merchandise exchanges without both a sales receipt and shopping bag. We've had a serious problem with shoplifting in this store," he adds, basically accusing us without saying it. See, now he's pissed me off.

"That's bullshit," I say, losing my cool. "I've been in here plenty of times, and I've seen other customers return merchandise without either. Just admit it, you think I stole this bag and have the nerve to bring it back here for money."

"Well, I didn't say that," he says, smiling a slick grin. "But if and when you find the receipt, you're more than welcome to return the gift." He and the saleslady look victorious as Mickey and I admit defeat and retreat toward the food court.

"Punk-ass bitches," Mickey says loud enough for them to hear as we head out the department store and into the busy mall. "I told you to keep the damned bag." I laugh.

"Yeah, yeah," I say, still unconvinced of her last statement. I'm just going to have to get the receipt from Jeremy, which ain't going to be pretty. "You want a lemonade? My treat," I offer as we glide up the tall escalator. This mall has the prettiest landscaping I've ever seen. It feels like I'm inside a greenhouse with all the tall plants and bright light throughout.

"Sounds good." As we step off and get in line at Hot Dog On a Stick, I get a strange feeling that someone's watching me. I turn around and see Misty, Nellie, Tania, Laura, KJ and the rest of South Central hanging out in the food court. Just what we need, more drama.

"You see them tricks over there hating?" Mickey says, sharing my view. "I need to continue Nellie's ass-whooping while I have the chance." But before Mickey makes a move, Misty's already on her way over to us. Nellie gets a worried look on her face, and now I know something's about to go down.

"What's up, y'all?" Misty says, trying to make small talk. With a mouth as big as hers, that will always be an impossible mission.

"What's up is that I saw you and Nellie chatting in the office yesterday," I say, diffusing any chance she has of gaining Mickey's trust. "What was that all about?"

"Damn, Jayd, why are you so suspicious all the time?" Misty says, rolling her neck and causing her long curly hair to whip from one side of her round behind to the other. KJ must be having a field day getting her sprung on him.

"Because she knows you, Misty," Mickey says, stepping out of line and toward her. "So spill it. What's up with Nellie?" As I order our drinks, Mickey pulls Misty off to the side and gets her version of the latest scoop, while Nellie watches from across the way.

"Speak up a little bit. It's busy in here," I say, handing Mickey the ice-cold drink while Misty continues her exposé.

"Well, like I said," Misty continues, not even trying to be discreet. This girl can't be trusted as anyone's true friend; Misty's too caught up in the glory of being the gossip queen of South Bay. Like Nellie's crown, it is a fictional honor admired only by the bored and delusional. "When Mickey came into the office a couple of weeks ago to clear her absences, Nellie let it slip in front of Mr. Langley, the assistant principal over attendance, that she saw you and Nigel sneak off campus, and he's investigating your and Nigel's absences as we speak. Y'all are in some deep shit if he finds out the truth—especially you, Mickey."

"Slip, my ass," Mickey says with venom dripping from her words.

"Mickey, wait," I say, holding her back from going after Nellie. "Look at the messenger before you go over there. It's Misty." I cut my eyes at my doppelgänger. Misty loves this, and she also loves the fact that, for once, no one's out to beat her ass. But I'm sure it's only a temporary shift in the atmosphere. Misty's always got enemies, even if right now they're nowhere to be found.

"Do you really think she made all that up? Nellie's been dying to get back at me for being with Nigel," Mickey says, looking me in the eye and seeing the truth for herself. I didn't tell her about Nellie's suspicious behavior yet because I wanted to get all my facts straight before coming to her, unlike Misty, who's just out for blood. KJ, Shae and the rest of the folks look our way as Mickey's voice rises, causing all chatter to cease. Nellie, hearing Mickey's words, begins to walk away, with her new crew right behind her. But she can't get away from Mickey this time.

"Hey, Nellie, can I have a word with you?" Mickey says, walking toward the escalator and blocking Nellie's escape attempt, with me right behind her. Laura and Tania back up; they don't want any part of this mess.

"What is it, Mickey? I'm kind of in a rush," Nellie says, sounding more like Tania every day. Before Nellie can work up the nerve to say anything else, Mickey flings her extra-large lemonade in Nellie's face and slaps her down to the ground. Here we go.

"Damn," the onlookers say in unison. As Nellie tries to regain her footing on the slippery floor, Mickey pushes her back down, talking mad shit. All the crowd's oohs and aahs can be heard throughout the otherwise silent space.

"Mickey, stop before you really hurt her," I say as I try to hold Mickey back with my free hand. She may have wasted her lemonade, but I'm not wasting mine.

"Would you feel the same way if your ex-best friend ratted you out?" she says. And she's right, I have wanted to kill Misty several times in the couple of years I've known her. But I still wouldn't do it like this, especially not in the same mall that just accused us of shoplifting. Speaking of which, here comes security now. Damn, just what we need, more mall employees in our business.

"What's going on here?" the guards say, breaking up the crowd that's encircled us. "Is everyone okay?" Nellie's regained her composure but still looks terrified and betrayed. Laura and Tania didn't even help her get up off the ground. What kind of friends does she think they are to her?

"No," Tania says, jumping in the middle of the circle, ready to tell all. "That girl attacked my friend." She points at Mickey, who already can't see straight through her rage. All she needs is another target.

"That's a lie," I say, forced to defend my friend as everyone else remains quiet, waiting to see what will happen next. Tania's charges are serious and could do more than get Mickey suspended or expelled. She could end up in jail over this bull, and that's not happening today. "This girl fell and slipped, and my friend tried to help her up, but it just got twisted around. Isn't that right, Nellie?" I say, looking from Nellie to Mickey, waiting for her reply. If she knows what's good for her, Nellie will go with my story and deflate this situation before it gets even more out of control.

"You're lying," Laura says, adding her two cents of loyalty to the queen of her hive. I hope they both get what they have coming to them. If Tania weren't pregnant, I'd jump her ass right now myself.

"Well, miss, it's your call," the brawly guard says to a shell-shocked Nellie. She can't speak and knows better than to say a word against Mickey to her face. I know Nellie hasn't forgotten where we all live. She can play that White-girl role at school. But when we get back to Compton, her fake-ass homies will be nowhere around, not that they're much good to her anyway.

"Nellie, say something," Tania says, egging her on. Even Misty's on the tip of her toes from the tension in the room.

"Well, if you're not going to say anything, there's nothing much I can do but get this mess cleaned up," he says, leaving the scene and summoning the cleaning crew to remove the evidence. Just as I predicted, Nellie hasn't completely lost her mind. But this is far from over. I know Mickey's going to have a field day planning her revenge on Nellie. How stupid could Nellie be to think that she could replace loyal friends after the fitting of her crown? Doesn't she know it takes time to find homies like me and Mickey, especially with her finicky ass? But like I said before, if she crossed Mickey, there would be nothing much I could do to protect her. So I hope she knows what she's doing because Mickey's out for blood and Nellie's is all that'll do.

Mama's busy with a witch hunt of her own sorts, so I know she won't have too much time to chat, and she had a hair appointment today. But I need to get some advice about this one. I don't want either of my friends to get hurt, but this has got to be put to rest, and fast.

When Mickey drops me off, Mama's screaming can be heard all the way down the block. Luckily Mickey was too absorbed in her own fire to hear the one going on inside my house. I hate when Mama gets like this. And usually Tuesdays are her chill days, after Netta's finished working her magic on Mama's head. But from the sound of it, Mama's head is anything but cool.

"Goddamnit, I've told you lazy–ass fools to stay the hell off my white couch," she says. Oh, Lord I hope no one took the plastic off her couch. My uncles do that sometimes, looking for change. Usually they put it back without her noticing too much. But something must've happened to piss her off like this.

"Lynn Mae, shut the hell up about that damned couch," Daddy says from outside. He's the only one who would dare talk back to Mama. "It's one stain, and I'm sure you can get it out." Now, why did Daddy have to go and say that? I think I'll just stay on the porch until this blows over. It's too much energy for me to take right now, especially after keeping Nellie and Mickey from an all-out brawl. I've done enough refereeing for one afternoon.

"Are you going to clean it up? Huh, Lee?" Mama yells out the back door. Now he's done it. When she gets to yelling outside, there's no calming her down. My mom thinks it has something to do with menopause. But to hear Daddy tell it, Mama's always been a hothead. I guess that's where I get it from, although my fire's a little spark compared to hers.

"Hell, no, I'm not cleaning it up," Daddy says, almost laughing. If he and Mama didn't argue, they'd barely communicate. I think he gets a kick out of pushing her buttons.

"Well, then, I guess you don't have shit to say about it then, do you?" Mama says, slamming the kitchen door. "And who left the beans on the stove uncovered? Do you like eating flies in your food?" she says, taking the top off the table and placing it on the large pot. It's then she notices a cake on her kitchen table, and Mama hasn't baked all week. I can see her look of recognition from my spot outside and decide it's time for me to intervene. I know that face: it must be from one of Daddy's church groupies.

"What the hell is this pound cake doing in here?" Mama says, picking up the heavy sweet and reopening the back door, tossing it outside to Daddy.

"Lynn Mae, what the hell!" Daddy screams, no longer amused by Mama's tantrum as he bends down to pick the pieces off the ground. Lemon pound cake is his favorite dessert.

"I told you not to bring any food in here from those church hussies!" Mama yells, slamming the door behind her. "This is my kitchen and my house. Don't be bringing no other heffa's nothing up in here, you hear me, Reverend James!" And with that final lethal slur, Mama goes to her room, shutting the door for the evening, I'm sure. She'll be in there all night praying and chanting for help with her temper, as she always does after she's vented like this.

I guess I'll have to wait until tomorrow to talk to her about my drama. Tonight I'll concentrate on cooling down all the hot energy around me by studying my lessons. Mama's going to give Netta a head cleansing tomorrow, and I need to be prepared to assist. Maybe she'll even let us do one on her. If anyone needs to cool off other than Mickey, it's Mama. And I need her to have a clear head to help me out of this madness. There's no replacing Mama's wisdom when it gets this bad.

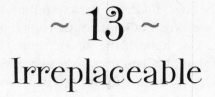

~ 13 ~

Irreplaceable

"So don't you ever for a second get to thinking/
You're irreplaceable."

—BEYONCÉ

Even after working in the spirit room all night chopping spinach and preparing the other ingredients that I could, I still didn't come up with any solutions to my problems. Some things only Mama can fix. So how am I going to ask Jeremy for the receipt for my return? The last thing we need is another issue in our new relationship. We already have enough to deal with as it is.

"Hey, lady," Jeremy says, reaching across the passenger's seat to open my door. "Jump in. I've got to head back home and grab my AP portfolio for the meeting after school." I take a seat and shut the door.

"Well, thank goodness you live up the street," I say. If I left my school work at home I'd simply be assed out for real. By the time I'd reach home and back, school would be over.

"Yeah, it has its perks," he says, smirking at me as we ride up the hill along with everyone else. It must be nice living in these huge houses with their fancy lawns, even if there's still family chaos to deal with. Well, I guess there's no time like the present to get back to the matter at hand.

"So, Jeremy," I say, not sure which issue to bring up first. I want to know exactly what's up with his dad before approaching the matter of the purse. Depending on how far we get and what he says, I'll know how to tell him I'm returning his gift. "Can we finish talking about your daddy and Black girls?" I say, making light of the heavy topic. I can tell by the way he's tightening his jaw that he was hoping to avoid the topic indefinitely. But it's too important to me to just let it go.

"Jayd, what difference does it make? You're with me, not him. I love you for who you are, not what you are, and I wish you could just be happy with that," he says. Jeremy does sound sincere, but the pain in his voice is too deep for me to ignore.

"Jeremy, that's all well and fine," I say, stroking his leg while he pulls up to the front of the school to drop me off. "But it makes a huge difference to me. This is the problem I have with Mrs. Bennett, Mrs. Peterson and other ignorant people who hate on me and my sistahs because of our strength." Jeremy rolls his eyes as though he's heard my speech before. But I continue anyway because it obviously hasn't sunk in yet.

"I'm serious. This isn't funny to me, and I want to know exactly what I'm dealing with the next time I see your father." Finally taking me seriously, Jeremy looks at me and spills the truth.

"My dad doesn't like Black women because he says they're too loud, bossy and rude." I'm a little taken aback by his confession but satisfied nonetheless.

"Then how did all his sons end up with Black women?" I ask. According to Ms. Toni, the Weiner boys are notorious for dealing with girls that aren't White.

"I don't know, really. I guess it's just one of those things. But for the record, me and my brothers like women, not just Black women," he says, his signature smile gleaming in the morning sun. And I like men; however, I do prefer the brothas overall. But Jeremy doesn't need to know all that.

"Okay, so what does this have to do with Tania? She's not Black, she's Persian." Jeremy's smile disappears as students start to walk up the path toward school. What is he hiding from me? "Jeremy, what is it? You can tell me anything, I promise," I say, holding his hand with my left hand and turning his face toward me with my other.

"Look, Jayd, I keep telling you some things are better left alone," Jeremy says. "You know Tania's pregnant, you know she's engaged to someone else and you know I'm not going to have anything to do with the baby. Isn't that enough? I have to go so I can get back before the bell rings," he says, kissing me gently on the mouth, making me almost forget about the receipt. I'll get it later. Right now, I want to stay in the bliss of ignorance as I long as I can. Whatever he doesn't want to tell me is big. And I don't know when we'll have the opportunity to kiss like this again.

When I make it into the partially empty main hall, I see Ms. Toni and Mrs. Bennett exchanging words by the ASB room up ahead of my locker. I wonder what that's all about. Out of all the staff at South Bay, these are the main arch enemies and each equally lethal in their own way. I better go over there before Ms. Toni has Mrs. Bennett's bleached-blond head for breakfast.

"Hey, Ms. Toni," I say, stepping up to her side as Mrs. Bennett's frown turns to a sinister smile. This is one twisted broad; I still don't understand how Jeremy and his crew love her so much. One of the main reasons I can't wait to graduate is just so I can get away from her.

"Hey, Jayd," Ms. Toni says through a forced smile. "It's nice to see your bright face."

"Jayd," Mrs. Bennett says. I love that she doesn't even pretend to like me. It makes it that much easier for me to hate her. "I think I'll leave the two of you alone now." Mrs. Bennett walks toward the front door. "And, Ms. Toni, remember what I said. Good teachers are irreplaceable." I wonder where she parks her broomstick before landing her wicked ass on campus.

"What was that all about?" I ask before we start walking back toward my locker. The bell's about to ring, and I know Ms. Toni has to get to her class, too.

"Oh, you know there's always something political going on at this school. That woman makes the hairs on the back of my neck stand straight up," Ms. Toni says. It must be something big to make her this upset. She's always telling me to be cool, even when dealing with this school's administration. Now it looks like she's the one who needs to chill.

"Whatever it is, I'm sure you'll find a way around it," I say, opening my locker as Ms. Toni looks off into the distance, staring at nothing in particular.

"Everything isn't that simple. Do you know how hard it is to find good teachers?" Ms. Toni says. "And then to keep those same good teachers from working at good schools like this one—because teachers that need to retire won't—just makes my blood boil." What the hell is she talking about?

"Ms. Toni, what's going on? Who's retiring?" I say, slamming my locker shut. I know I'm going to be late if I don't get going, but it sounds like Ms. Toni needs to talk.

"Oh, Jayd, I wish I could say something, but I can't," she says, looking just as defeated as she did when we went up against Mrs. Bennett together. It makes me feel sad that I can't be of more help to her. "Just pray for a little consciousness at this school." She walks off toward her office and leaves me to ponder her last statement. Maybe there's something I can do to help her situation after all. Besides, all good things start with a little positive thought, and that I can get to work on right now.

* * *

After yesterday's mall drama, I was grateful for the long day and distracting AP meetings. Nellie was absent, and Mickey and Nigel were in the office all day, explaining their absences, I assume. With Jeremy in his meeting after school, I had a lot of time on the bus to think about everything that's been going on lately. Is it that easy to replace the people in our lives?

Mama tossing Daddy's cake yesterday really hit home with me. She wasn't upset just because Daddy's eating someone else's cake; it hurt her to think that Daddy had replaced her with another woman. I know how she feels. It also hurts that Nellie replaced me and Mickey without as much as a bat of her mascara-coated eyelashes. It also hurts to think that Jeremy could think that buying me an expensive bag would ever replace me knowing the truth. Right now, I'm not feeling too hot about myself, and I really need Mama's guidance. I hope she's chilled out from yesterday's festivities before she gives Netta a *rogación de cabeza*. If not, all her negative energy could end up in Netta's head, and that wouldn't be good for Netta or Netta's clients.

When I get home, Daddy's outside polishing his baby-blue Cadillac El Dorado. I think he loves this car more than he loves Mama or their eleven children. My uncles are in the house watching television and fixing their dinner, as usual. When Mama does cleansings for her clients, she spends the whole day in the spirit room prepping for the ritual. I'm sure she already has my clean whites in the back with her, waiting for me to come help. I've already missed the major labor—cleaning the room, gathering the remaining herbs and plants, preparing the water. But I did help with some of the preparations last night while studying.

"Hey, there, tweet," Daddy says, looking up from his fun labor to give me a smile and quick peck. "Your mama's in her room with Netta," he says, pointing toward the backhouse behind the garage. If there was a full bathroom, I'm sure Mama would live out there all the time.

"Hey Daddy. You gone let me drive her when I get my license next month?" I say, caressing the spotless ride. I still haven't told my mom or Mama about my dad paying for my lessons. It keeps slipping my mind, but I'll get around to it soon enough.

"Girl, you know I don't let anybody drive my car," he says. I remember my uncle Junior took the car one night thinking Daddy would never find out. And he wouldn't have found out, but Jay couldn't wait to tell on Junior the next morning. Daddy kicked his ass all the way down the block and back over that one, permanently checking anyone who'd ever think of driving one of Daddy's cars again.

"I know, Daddy. I'm just teasing you," I say, kissing him on the cheek. How can he be sweet to me but so awful to Mama? "Daddy, can I ask you something?" Maybe he'll be truthful with me about his relationships with other women since I'm on the sidelines of their adult games, no matter how similar the playing field.

"Sure, tweet, what's on your mind?" I love it when he calls me my nickname. It's just between me and him; no one else has ever called me tweet, and he's never called me by any other name.

"Why do you want other women when you have Mama at home?" Stopping in his tracks, Daddy takes a deep breath and looks at me very sternly. Oh, shit, I knew I went too far when the words came out, but I had to ask. He looks back at the car and continues polishing before saying another word.

"This here is a nineteen seventy-five convertible Cadillac El Dorado. No matter how many new cars they come out with, there is no replacement for this vehicle. They don't make them like this anymore," he says, polishing the same spot for what must be the fiftieth time. Why is he talking about this damned car when I just asked him why he cheats on my grandmother? Before I can walk away, he continues his sermon, gluing me to my spot.

"Lynn Mae is the most beautiful woman I've ever seen," he says, entranced by his own movements. "When I first saw those fiery green eyes and that long black hair, I thought I'd died and gone to heaven. I vowed right then and there, if she'd be my wife, I'd never lay eyes on another woman again—ever."

"Well, what happened?" I say. I know Mama's looking at the wall clock and wondering where I am. It's already past five now, and I know there's still a lot of work to do for Netta. But I need to know what happens to make people feel like they can replace their loved ones or even friends, because a sistah's hella confused right now, and I need some answers.

"Time happened," he says wearily. "Shit happens, people talk, more shit happens and then, well, you disconnect and it all falls apart after that." Damn, that actually makes sense to me. In all my friendships, even with Misty, that's pretty much the same recipe for destruction I've experienced.

"But why stay together?" I say. "Especially for as long as you and Mama have been together?" I can't even stay with KJ or Jeremy for a couple of months, and they've been together for over thirty-five years.

"Tweet, no matter how many times you go out hunting, you always come back home. I could never leave your grandmother, not even if I wanted to. There's nobody else in the world I trust like that hotheaded woman back there. And Lynn Mae won't admit it, but she feels the same way. We love each other, no matter how it may appear to the outside world. And like the Bible says, love is patient, and I'm willing to wait for things to turn around, even it does take a lifetime."

"Well, all righty then," I say, taking Daddy's words to

heart. As much as it may appear that they hate each other, it looks like the onlookers, including me, are terribly wrong. I wonder if Mama knows how much she still means to Daddy. Maybe if she did, they'd be a little sweeter to each other. "I better get back there. And thanks for the talk," I say, leaving Daddy to his work and us to ours.

"No problem. And, tweet, no matter what happens in life, stay sweet. That is, after all, why I gave you your nickname," Daddy says, returning to his waxing.

"I thought it was because I looked like a little yellow bird when I was born," I say, repeating the story my mom told me.

"Well, that, too, but mostly because when your grandmother saw you for the first time, she said you were so sweet. In that baby talk of hers it sounded like tweet, and that's what stuck in my head." The rare times he's home, I love vibing with my grandfather. But I better get to the back before Mama sends Lexi after me.

"Where have you been, girl? I was starting to get worried," Mama says, filling the large tin basin with water and white flowers for Netta's bath. Netta must be inside grating her cocoa butter and concentrating on her prayers. The cleansing process starts in the mind, as my lessons stated last night. Nobody gives a head cleansing like Mama. "Go clean up and put your whites on, Jayd. We have a lot of work to do." Mama picks more roses from the bushes next to the miniature house. The scent of the flowers rises to my nose, making me feel calmer than I've felt all week. The term "soul work" must've originated with the Williams Women legacy because I always feel lifted when doing Mama's work.

"Are you feeling better?" I ask her. She looks like nothing ever happened. How can she be so forgiving all the time? I guess that family trait skipped both me and my mom.

"I feel good, girl. Now go get dressed and bring Netta out here with you when you're ready. Did you study the *rogación* ingredients and their purposes?" Mama asks, grilling me before I even have a chance to get in the door good.

"Yes, I did," I say as I walk into the tiny kitchen where Netta, also robed in white, sits at the table with a plate full of shredded cocoa butter in front of her. The soft Cuban drumbeats in the background massage my temples, inviting me into the sacred space. This is why I come home. I nod hello to Netta—who can only nod back, as during a cleansing the client is forbidden to speak—and head to the back of the breezy room. There are windows on each wall, leaving little privacy, but Mama's fixed that, too.

I take my whites off the hanger behind the bathroom door and go behind the Chinese screens to change; there's no room in the small washroom to even turn around in. Mama's maximized all the space in this room to perfection. It's amazing that she can fit everything in here that she does. None of her clients have ever complained about the cozy space or the prices Mama charges for her work, which I think isn't nearly enough. The only thing they ever say is that they feel the spirit in here, as do I.

"Are you ready?" I ask Netta as I take her by the arm and lead her out of the room, cocoa butter in hand.

"Jayd, help Netta kneel beside the basin and then go and bring me all the ingredients for an Ori cleansing," Mama says, confident I already memorized my lessons. Since we've been concentrating on the power of thoughts, all my lessons have been about one's Ori, or personal destiny. Osun, our deity, isn't even as powerful as an individual's Ori. Nothing can substitute the blessings of one's destiny when you really need to get something done.

I walk back into the kitchen and retrieve the soft black

soap I pounded last night, fresh spinach from our garden
and some red palm oil from the cabinet. When Mama sees
my loot, she looks at me, proud of my progress. I have to
admit, I'm kind of proud of myself for this one. Because the
lessons weren't all about Queen Califia, Osun or Maman but
also about other important elements of our way of life, I didn't
take it seriously at first. But now I see the value in the individual sections of Mama's spirit book, and I'm anxious to
learn more. This must be where my mom got bored and
stopped studying.

"Jayd, hold this sheet up so I can begin the cleansing,"
Mama says, handing me a kingsize white sheet to hide us
from any nosey onlookers along the exposed side of the wall.
Luckily we're shielded by fig trees and the garage on the
other side facing the house. But you never know who may
want to sneak a peak. Clients are always cleansed outside,
even Netta. I prefer to do my cleansings out here as well. But
Mama prefers we do ours inside to be closer to our family
shrines.

After we finish Netta's ceremony, her husband picks her
up while Mama and I clean up and catch up on yesterday's
happenings at school.

"Jayd, I know you don't want to help her, but you and I
both know that Nellie's in way over head with this one," she
says, sweeping the floor where a nesting Lexi lies. Oh, to be a
dog in Mama's world. "Mickey will eat her alive if her true enemies don't get to her first."

"I know," I say in total agreement. Nellie has crossed dangerous territory messing with her friend turned enemy. "I
don't understand how she thought Tania and them would
make better friends than me and Mickey. The girl's completely
lost her mind." I wash the rest of the ceremonial dishes be-

fore drying them off and return them to the counter. If people saw all the work Mama puts into her rituals, they'd give her at least double what she asks.

"It's not about who would make a better friend, Jayd," Mama says, taking a seat and stretching her legs under the table. Mama's been back here all day and still has more work to do before Halloween this weekend. I still haven't got my costume together. I'm going to raid my mom's closet as usual when I get there on Friday. Jeremy's going to take me straight there because he knows I have to get ready for the dance.

"Then what is it, because I don't get it. A crown can't be that serious," I say, joining her at the table. It's almost nine, and I've got mad homework due by the end of the week. Tomorrow will have to be another crunch day in the library if I'm going to get it all done.

"Oh, Jayd, some people don't know how good they've got it until it's gone," she says, sounding like she's not talking about my school problems at all. "I'm sure Nellie regrets everything she's done by now and wants to find her way back to y'all, but it's hard to admit when you're wrong."

"So you're saying we should just forgive her like she didn't betray us both?" I say. I can't believe Mama's giving me the "turn the other cheek" rationalization after all she's been through with frenemies. And although Mama may turn the other cheek, she never closes her eyes.

"No, I'm not saying be stupid, Jayd. I'm just saying try to put yourself in her shoes before you're so quick to write her off as your enemy. Real friends are hard to come by, no matter how stupid they may act sometimes. Mickey was right to smack her; I would've done the same thing," Mama says, her emerald eyes displaying the youth behind her gray hairs. "Sometimes it's better if a friend kicks your ass, rather than an enemy; the pain is out of love more so than hate. And sometimes that's what it takes to turn things around." Mama's right; I've been too soft about this whole thing. I need to concentrate on checking Nellie's ass first, Tania next. I need all my allies with me, and if I have to get rough, then that's what I'll have to do, no matter what Jeremy or his dad may think of how we sistahs handle our business.

~ 14 ~
Kick-Ass Boots

"One of these days these boots/
Are gonna walk all over you."

—NANCY SINATRA

After last night's festivities, I didn't have much time to study or do any homework, so I spent all my free time in the library today, which was cool. Mickey's in in-house suspension again for the next two days, and Nigel, because he's a football player, was given his sentence in the gym. I don't know how the school justifies lifting weights as a punishment. But that's part of the perks that come with being an athlete. All I know is I better get to Nellie before Mickey does and try to talk some sense into her. But with her playing the disappearing act, it's going to make it hard for me to do.

"Hey, Jayd, are you ready to go?" Jeremy says, surprising me at my locker. I guess now's as good a time as any to ask for the receipt so I can take back my purse. I hate to do it, especially since our relationship seems to be on thin ice. But I've got to stand up to him and let him know that, unlike other chicks he's used to dating, my principles aren't for sale.

"Yeah," I say, closing my locker and taking his hand. "Would you mind if we stopped by the mall on the way home?" I go in for the kill. "I need to take something back."

"Something like what," he says, looking at me suspiciously. "I haven't seen you sporting the new bag. Is there something wrong with it?" He sounds so sweet I almost chicken out. But I've got to be strong.

"The bag is beautiful," I say, momentarily envying Mickey's nonchalant attitude when it comes to material things. "But I can't keep it." My gold *J* bangle falls down my wrist as I slip my hand out of his and continue walking toward the exit; it reminds me that I've already been bought twice in our short relationship.

"Jayd, what's this all about?" Jeremy says, catching up to me and reclaiming my hand. He stops me in the now empty hall, turning me around to look him in the face. "Are you still upset with me because of what Tania said to you the other day?"

"Yes, but it's not just that," I say. "How can I get you to understand that although I appreciate your gifts, that's not what I want or need from a boyfriend." If Mickey could only hear me now, she'd probably have me committed to an insane asylum or something. Nellie, too, for that matter.

"What the hell!" Jeremy yells, letting out his frustrations and stealing my coined phrase. "You are the most difficult girl I've ever dated." He puts his hands over his head and squeezes the brim of his baseball cap. He looks like he wants to blow up, but he contains his anger.

"Well, judging by your exes, that's a compliment," I say. "Look, I'm not a simple bitch who can be deterred by the bling. And believe it or not, I actually like buying my own stuff; it makes me feel proud." I feel good about my stance, now that it's out in the open.

"Proud," he says, like he can't believe what I just said. "You feel proud spending your hard-earned money on a bag that I can buy without even thinking about how much it cost?" Now he sounds cocky. "That's stupid, Jayd. You should save your money to help your family or whatever it is you need to do with it."

"Help my family?" I ask. What is he talking about? "Who

told you my family needed help?" Has he been talking to Misty? That sounds like some shit she'd say. But I know better than that. He wouldn't even give that heffa the time of day after she ratted him out for selling weed on campus.

"Well, isn't that why you don't want me to see where you live? You're too embarrassed to have me over," he says, pissing me way the hell off. I knew he still wondered why I allowed him to take me only as far as the bus stop after school. But I didn't think he thought it was because I was poor. This dude is too much if he thinks he's rescuing me or something.

"No, fool, it's not because I'm embarrassed about my house," I say, punching him in the arm and walking through the back door of the hall. "I'm embarrassed to have you over," I add, finally letting it all hang out. "I don't want to get clowned for bringing the beach boy to the hood." I never would have told him my feelings in that way, but he pushed me, and now they're out.

"Okay, Jayd, if you say so," he says, following me through the quad and toward the bus stop. "But I think we both know the truth. That's why I didn't want to tell you what my dad thinks, because it's all about race, class and money, and that shit don't matter to me."

"If it doesn't matter to you so much," I say, speed walking up the hill, "then why did you take it upon yourself to think about my money for me, huh? Why not just give me the money if you think we need it so damn much?"

"Jayd, you're too proud for your own good," Jeremy says, sounding like he's my daddy. "You need to just relax and accept my attention. It also wouldn't hurt you to be a little grateful, too." This time he's gone too far.

"Who do you think you are? Captain Save-a-Ho or somebody?" I say.

"Who?" he asks, looking confused. I forget he won't get some of my jokes.

"Don't patronize me, Jeremy. You're so delusional, you actually thought I'd be silenced by a purse," I say, taking the expensive bag out of my backpack and throwing it at him. "Take the damned thing back yourself. I'm taking the bus back to my little poorhouse in Compton." I feel hotter than a tiny red chili pepper right about now.

"Jayd, I think you're overreacting just a bit!" Jeremy yells after me. But I don't care. He's got all kinds of stuff going on in his head about me that I never imagined. What the hell is really up? All I know is that these Timberlands are going to give me a blister by the time I get home. If I had known I was going to be walking this afternoon, I would've worn my Nikes. It's been only a few weeks and I've already become so spoiled by Jeremy and didn't even know it. The three bus rides and the walk home will do me some good.

I need to cool off before talking with Jeremy again because we have a lot of issues to get straight. All this time I thought he was falling in love with me because he thought I was strong and independent. But now I see I'm more like his charity case who comes with the added benefit of pissing off his dad. I hate to admit when I'm wrong, but I think I overlooked a lot about dating Jeremy. And to top it off, he's again not accompanying me to a school dance, leaving me vulnerable to Rah's advances, and I know he's going to be there waiting for his chance to get at me again, which now I'm ready to admit I'm looking forward to. At least Rah's real with me always, no matter how much it hurts.

With Mickey and Nigel still on lockdown and Nellie avoiding me like the plague, today was very quiet. Jeremy and I have hardly spoken a word to each other all day, and that's just fine with me. I think we're both feeling like we may have rushed into this relationship without really getting to know each other. I don't know that we will remain friends if we break up or if we would've ever really been friends in the first place. Sometimes I'm attracted to people I don't really like. And I don't know what to do about any of those people in my life right now.

My mom picked me up from school since she had the day off today. She doesn't take personal days often, but she and Karl are going to Las Vegas tonight, so she had to go shopping, get her hair whipped and do her nails. By the time we get back to her house, I'll have just enough time left with her to pick out my Halloween outfit and send her off, leaving me to get ready alone. Mickey's going to pick me up at eight so we can be fashionably late to the festivities.

"So, have you decided what you're going as?" my mom says, turning onto Century Boulevard, just minutes away from her house.

"Not really. I know I want to go as Coffy, but I'm not sure which scene," I say, referring to one of our favorite movies. When I was a little girl, my mom used to watch all the Black films from the seventies: *Super Fly, Shaft, Foxy Brown* and *Coffy*, just to name a few. They're our own version of super-heroes from the hood.

"Oh, I have the cutest nurse's outfit from last year's Halloween party at your aunt Vivica's house. You can wear that if you want," she says, giving me a naughty wink. I've always picked my costumes out of hand-me-downs, unlike the majority of students at South Bay, who spend more on a costume than I would on clothes for the entire semester.

"Mom, this is high school, not the strip club," I say. Sometimes my mom forgets I'm still a teenager. I know a lot of these girls out here be letting it all hang out, but I'm not one of them.

"Girl, it's classy, I promise." As we turn onto Arbor Vitae, almost home, I see children already out with an assortment of plastic faces and pumpkins for collecting candy. My mom has never been into trick-or-treating, so I doubt there's any candy for them waiting at her door. She used to take me and my cousin Jay to the mall, and we'd walk around collecting candy from the various stores, and then we'd spend the rest of the night at Daddy's church, where they always had something going on for the kids. I miss those days.

"Okay, I'll check it out when we get home," I say. One benefit of going as a nurse who kicks ass on the side is that I'll be dressed for the part of helping out those in need, because I'm sure there's going to be plenty of drama to go around tonight—blood, worms and all.

"These boots are fierce," I say, taking from her jam-packed closet the red leather boots behind the clean white outfit covered with a plastic bag.

"Yeah, they really make the costume." And she's right. It's a long nurse's dress with buttons all the way down and a slit on the right side. The small nurse's hat with the red cross on it is the only thing medical about this outfit. "I told you it was classy," she says, taking the boots out of the bag and placing them on the floor beside my feet. She takes out her small carry-on luggage and starts to pack for her overnight adventure.

"Okay, but what am I going to do with these?" I say, looking at the three-inch heels, knowing I'm setting myself up for disaster if I wear those things.

"Oh, Jayd, stop being so shy," she says, taking one of the boots and putting it on. She's stunning and can work the hell out of any shoes, unlike me. "It's all in your hips, see?" She models the perfect sassy strut in the mirror.

"Yeah, I can see myself falling on my face in the gym." As the image of me sliding across the basketball court enters my mind, so does the one of Nellie having a mouthful of worms for dessert. Sensing my discomfort, my mom walks over to me, holding my face in her hands.

"Oh, Jayd, why didn't you tell me you had another dream? And such an awful image," she says, seeing what I'm seeing for herself. My mom's powers trip me out. But it seems to me she's more in control of them than I am of mine, even without finishing her lessons with Mama.

"Mom, how do you keep from reading my thoughts when you don't want to?" I ask. My mom sits down on the bed next to me, patting my thigh.

"It's all about willpower. Remember how somewhere in the spirit book it talks about mind over matter and how your Ori is the one who can help you before anyone else?" she says, reminding me of the ceremony we just did for Netta a couple days ago. "Well, that's how I control my thoughts creeping into your head—by allowing my Ori to take over, instead of me forcing the issue of not wanting to think about your shit," she says, sounding more like Mama than she'll ever admit to.

"So you're saying I can learn to control my dreams?" Imagine that. If I could control what I dream about and when, I wouldn't know what to do with myself. Or if I could change the outcome without having to go through it in the real world, now that would be tight.

"Not necessarily," my mom says, bursting my bubble. "But you can control the way they affect you. For example," she says, sliding the long boot off of her thin leg, "Nellie eating worms shouldn't affect your feelings. You should be able to see that and see the final outcome of the situation you want and not feel a thing. Separate your vision from your emotions, Jayd. Then and only then will you have a little more control over your powers." Damn, I never thought about it like that. Have my feelings toward Nellie in some way caused this situation to occur in my dreams, and now in real life?

Yes, more than likely they have, my mom answers me in her head while getting up to take a shower. "But once you get the hang of them, you'll be able to help people just like Maman and Mama do. I have faith in your abilities, little girl," she says, taking the cutest purple bra and panties out of her top dresser drawer and heading into the bathroom.

I need to catch up with Mickey before she gets here. I tried calling Nellie several times throughout the day, but, as usual, she's not answering her phone.

"What's up, Mickey?" I say into the phone. It sounds like I've interrupted her doing God only knows what. I've learned never to ask, where Mickey's concerned.

"What's up, Jayd? I'm catching up with my man. Can I call you back later?" I can hear him in the background grilling her, and it doesn't sound like anything nice.

"Yeah, sure. But real quick: who are you going as to the party?" I have to make sure she's not planning on wearing the same thing as me.

"Pam Grier."

"What! So am I!" I shout into the phone. I should've known. The few Black girls at the school will probably all be her in some way. She is the Black shero of the seventies.

"Well, then, we'll be twins," she says, trying to rush me off the phone.

"No, that ain't going to work. I'm wearing a nurse's outfit, so just don't wear anything white," I say.

"Fine, Jayd. I'll see you in a couple hours," she says, hanging up the phone. I still need to do my hair before she gets here, and my mom being in the bathroom isn't helping, but she's leaving soon. Then I'll have the place to myself and can hook up my do. I know my mom still has her Afro wig around here somewhere, and I can braid my hair up underneath. Then I won't have to worry about it for work tomorrow either. I'm looking forward to playing dress up, especially in my fly-ass red boots. I need all the power I can get, even if it's all in my head.

* * *

Because Mickey and I both decided to go as Pam Grier, she has now assured me she'll go as Foxy Brown. Nigel and Raheem are coming to the dance, as expected, but keeping their costumes on the low. I'm sure they'll look good no matter what they wear. And I know, with it being a seventies party, they're both going to be pimped out.

"Damn, girl, you look almost as good as I do," Mickey says when she arrives, her pink Regal shiny from the fresh wax her man must've put on it. I'm surprised she's in such a good mood after what I overheard on the phone earlier. Knowing her, that's not the only thing that got waxed.

"You don't look so bad yourself," I say, commenting on her short skirt, low-cut blouse and fly-ass straight wig hanging down her back. "I wasn't sure you were going to make it." I get in the car.

"I know. My man's tripping hard. But I got him to shut before I left," she says, smiling. This girl is too much for me sometimes. We need Nellie back to buffer us out. Without her, it's just too much heat around here.

"TMI Mickey: way too much information," I say as she pulls off toward the beach. It's a breezy evening but not too cool. I have on my mother's red wool wrap, which matches my outfit perfectly. I hope I can get to Nellie before she takes a bite of that apple and gets the treat of her life. I still have to convince Mickey to help, even if she does consider Nellie to be enemy number one right now.

"Whatever, girl. You better learn some tricks from me and save your little relationships while you can," Mickey says, putting her long airbrushed acrylic nails through her wig with one hand as she taps on the steering wheel with the other.

"The only relationship I'm worried about saving is the one between you, me and Nellie."

"Oh, hell, no, Jayd. I know you're not serious about that girl," she says, rolling her eyes at me. I see she hasn't cooled off a bit.

"Look, Mickey, she's our girl. She's been taken over by the dark side, and it's our job to get her back."

"You sound like one of those goddamned White-ass horror flicks," she says, turning onto Aviation toward PCH. The nightlife is always cracking out here.

"You know what, Mickey, you'll thank me for it later," I say, convincing myself that she'll change her mind. "Besides, I can't do it alone. I need your help."

"It's always the ones who want to help that get killed off first in those movies," she says, unrelenting in her judgment. No matter what Mickey says, we're getting our friend back tonight, and we're also going to find out who our real friends are and who are just enemies in sheep's clothing.

~ 15 ~
Trick or Treat

*"My night nurse/
Only you alone can quench this Jah thirst."*

—GREGORY ISAACS

These White folks go all out for their parties. There's a disco ball dripping blood in the center of the gymnasium ceiling, hanging from the scoreboard. Everyone's taken their costumes to a gory edge, making me and Mickey look like virgins. I think we all watched similar movies because everyone's either got on an Afro, a long wig or some extra-high boots. But none of these folks look as bad as we do, and I know it, because all eyes are instantly on us when we walk in the room.

"Mickey," I hear Nigel say as we enter the crowded gym. "Damn, girl, you look good," he says, grabbing her by the waist and kissing her cheek. They look cute as a couple, but it's too bad that—like this gym turned haunted house—it's all an illusion.

"You don't look so bad yourself, *Super Fly.*" And Mickey's right. Nigel looks damn good in his cream-colored three-piece suit and hat with the leather boots to match.

"Damn, girl, you want to join my stable?" he says, sounding like the pimp he wishes he was.

"You already got one more fly girl than you need," I say, instinctively eyeing the packed room for Rah.

"Your boy's not here yet," Nigel says, reading my mind. "I

don't know why you frontin'; y'all just need to go on and get back together," he says, stepping behind Mickey and claiming his spot for the evening. But I've got other plans for his main chick.

"Whatever, Nigel. Me and Mickey have business to handle. We'll be right back," I say, taking Mickey by the arm and leading her toward the cauldron where Nellie and her girls are hanging out. Nellie looks cute in her *Wonder Woman* costume, even if there are ten more girls in the room wearing the same outfit. Judging from her constant nose wiggling, pointy hat and broom, I'm assuming Tania is Samantha from *Bewitched,* and, just as my dream predicted, she has crossed the outfit with a hooker's clothes. Laura's the plainest version of *Catwoman* I've ever seen, and Reid thinks he's the shit in his *Batman* gear. It's truly a star-studded event.

"Jayd, where the hell are you taking me?" Mickey says, looking back at Nigel as I strut across the floor, ready to start something with Nellie for the last time.

"We're going to have a chat with our girl," I say, my heart pounding harder the closer we get to the scene. Nellie's third in line for the apple bob, and I know Tania's treat will be waiting for her in the cold water if I don't do something about it. These boots make me feel powerful, just as my mom predicted, and they're also turning a lot of heads, including KJ's and his boys', pissing off Misty and her girls. It does our souls good to play dress up, especially in characters that may serve as our alter egos. Speak of the devil, I spot Chance in line behind Nellie, dressed as John Travolta in *Saturday Night Fever:* tight pants, gold chains and all.

"Unless I'm talking while whipping her ass, I don't have anything to say to the trick," Mickey says, turning around and heading back toward Nigel, who's in pursuit of us, with Rah right by his side. I have to pause and catch my breath as Rah's image knocks the wind out of me. He looks stunning in all black as he portrays one of my favorite characters, *Shaft*, with his hair in an Afro like mine. Damn, he looks good in leather.

"Jayd, I don't know how you can convince yourself that you love Jeremy when you have all this fine-ass Black man right here in front of you," Mickey says, gesturing toward our approaching boys. "I don't care if he's got that little trifling girlfriend at his school, that's your man, girl, and you better claim him while you still can."

"Mickey, is he going somewhere?" I say. She sounds like there's a shortage of good Black men around or something, and I'm not buying that. "And him having a girlfriend may be okay with you, but I take commitment seriously," I say, bracing myself for Rah's touch. He wears P. Diddy's cologne better than its namesake, I imagine.

"You look good, Nurse Coffy," Rah says, swooping me up in his arms and kissing my neck. Misty, KJ and crew all look over at us from the bleachers where they've relocated South Central for the evening. They've decided to go as the Black Panthers, all wearing big Afros, black leather jackets and dashikis. Now see, that's what I'm talking about. If they weren't so stank all the time, I'd be down with the solidarity they have as a clique. Why can't me and my girls stay as tight as they appear?

"Thank you, Shaft. You don't look so bad yourself," I say as he puts me back on my feet and looks down at me. "Isn't your school having a Halloween function of its own?" I know Westingle is just as active as South Bay, and Rah and Nigel have enough school spirit for both campuses.

"Yeah, and we're going to hit that one up later," he says. "Nurse, I think I'm feeling a little hot." Rah grabs my hand and puts it on his forehead, making Mickey and Nigel laugh. "Can you cool me off?"

"Rah, shut up and stop molesting my hand," I say, snatching away from his grasp and playfully hitting him on his arm.

"Mickey and I were on our way to handle something. We'll be right back." I reclaim Mickey from Nigel and march toward our intended target. Boys can be so distracting sometimes.

"Hey, wait up. We want to watch," Nigel says as he and Rah follow us to the cauldron line.

"Jayd, I already told you I'm done with Nellie. I can never trust her again, and so to me, she might as well be dead," Mickey says. But I can't let it go this easily.

"Mickey, out of all the times Nellie has had your back and you hers, how can you give up on her so easily?" Noticing our approach, Tania tries to rush China, who's in front of her in line. But she just can't seem to catch an apple in the dark container full of water, giving us more time to rescue Nellie.

"Because I've never turned on her like this, Jayd," Mickey says loud enough to quiet some nearby people, including Nigel and Rah. "This is the worst shit a friend can do. Why can't you get that?"

"Because I believe in forgiveness, Mickey, especially when it's someone you love," I say, looking at an intense Rah as he stares straight through me. I know we're sharing the same memory of him cheating on me with my cousin and then our entire junior high crew temporarily turning on me as a result of me fronting on them both at school. But that was a long time ago.

"Well, that's you. I believe in letting bitches be," Mickey says, staring at Nellie, who's now heavily engrossed in our conversation from where she's standing. Tania nervously tries to push the girl in front of her out of the way, but to no avail. China's determined to get herself an apple if it's the last thing she does. She's probably got the munchies, as usual.

"Mickey, we don't have time for this," I say, noticing Tania's loose sleeve with the green apple sticking out underneath. "Nellie's always been the clueless, material one in the crew, so stop acting like you don't know her as well as I do, if not better."

"Listen to your girl, Mickey," Nigel says, putting his two cents in, which may be enough to convince her. "You can't let good friends slip away." He strokes her bare arms.

"But she turned us in," Mickey wines, almost defeated. "You want me to just let that go?"

"Well, technically, it was Misty. Nellie just verified the info," Nigel says, giving me some news I didn't know. I've been so wrapped up in my own drama, I forgot to follow up with Mickey about their in-house suspensions this week.

"Misty? Why am I not surprised," I say, noticing Rah hasn't taken his eyes off me as he stands behind Nigel, waiting for our next move. The party is really getting hyped around us as the deejay begins to play old disco music, getting everyone up on the dance floor.

"Because you know how she is," Nigel says, still trying to win Mickey over. "Come on, baby." Nigel kisses Mickey's nose and then her mouth. These two have no shame in their cheating game.

"Fine, whatever," Mickey says, kissing him back. "But, Jayd, we're even after this," she adds, ready to take over Tania's world with me. Two different yet equally powerful versions of the closest thing we've got to a Black female superhero in the seventies to save our Oreo counterpart; now, that's power.

"Come on, girl, let's go rescue Wonder Woman," I say, ready to give Tania a dose of her own nasty medicine.

"Oh, no, not the ghetto girls again," Tania says, causing her crowd to chuckle. But by the time we're done with her, I'll be the last one laughing.

"Tania, what's up your sleeve?" I say, walking toward her, ready to expose her for the twisted trick she is. Acting as her bodyguard, Reid steps in front of her, almost knocking down an irritated Chance.

"I can't let you get too close, Jayd. You're known to have quite a temper, and Tania's in a fragile condition," he says, sounding like the chivalrous knight he isn't.

"Reid, get out of my way before I step on you with my heels," I say, ready to kick his ass if need be. But noticing me and Mickey's backup, he stands down and leaves me to handle what I came here for.

"Jayd, what are you talking about?" Tania says, feigning shock.

"The apple up your sleeve, Tania. Give it here," I say, reaching for her arm as she steps back out of my reach.

"Is it a crime to bring your own fruit?" she says, taking the large green treat out of her clothing, causing everyone to fall silent.

"How did you know she had it?" Nellie asks, looking at me suspiciously. I haven't shared my secret with her yet, but she should know me well enough by now to trust my intuition, no matter how crazy it may seem.

"I saw it from across the room. Nellie, she was going to plant that apple for you. There's something wrong with it, I just know it," I say, trying to reason with my fallen girl without giving up all my secret knowledge.

"You're lying," Laura says, coming to Tania's defense. I don't know why she's pledged her blind allegiance to her, but Laura can see no wrong in any of Tania's actions, ever. "Tania would never do anything like that to a friend."

"Nellie, don't listen to her," Tania says, recasting her spell of deceit. "She's just jealous of you, Nellie, you know this." Nellie again hardens her feelings and turns away from me, as though to say she's had enough. Well, so have I.

"If I'm lying, Tania, then take a bite," I say, calling her bluff. I trust my dreams more than I trust this trick's word.

"I don't have to prove anything to you," she says, turning away from the cauldron and heading toward the exit.

"No? Then have Laura take a bite," I say, daring her friendship skills. I know this heffa's twisted, but let's see just how far she'll go to save face. "If I'm wrong, which I'm not, then give the apple to Laura and let's see who the real liar is around here."

"Jayd, we are not going to play your silly little game," Tania says. But, having drawn a crowd with China, Misty and everyone else surrounding us now chanting, "Bite, Bite," Tania can't get away this time.

"Give her the apple or bite it yourself, Tania. That's the only way you're getting out of here," I say, Mickey stepping up right beside me. I know Tania doesn't want to challenge me and my girl. If Tania thinks I'm a bit much, then she ain't seen nothing yet.

"Food makes me nauseous," she says, playing off her pregnancy for sympathy. This girl is something else, and I feel sorry for her baby. Having money doesn't guarantee mental stability or a great childhood, no matter what she or Jeremy may think.

"Give it to me," Laura says, snatching the shiny green object from Tania's grasp and inspecting it. "I trust my friends." Before Reid or Nellie can say anything, Laura bites into the apple, making a loud crunch sound ripple through the now silent gym. Everyone's waiting to see what'll happen next.

"See? Nothing," Laura says, chewing the piece of fruit in her mouth and turning the other portion toward the onlookers, myself included. Was my dream wrong? But just as I begin to doubt myself, tiny worms start to surface from the bitten flesh, eliciting a loud gasp of shock and disgust from the crowd. Noticing their reaction, Laura spits the apple into her hand and sees the same thing.

"You sick bitch!" Reid screams at Tania, who's looking for a quick escape route. But I ain't done with her yet. I know she's probably going to leave for New York soon after this incident, especially if Jeremy signs the papers. So I need the full confession, in front of Nellie and everyone else, before she goes.

"Do you see now what kind of chick this is, Nellie?" I say, screaming at my friend as Laura gulps down a cup of red punch Reid brought her. What a Halloween treat she got. "How could you leave us to kick it with her?"

"Because Tania told her if she didn't become our new pledge, she'd put the picture of her changing on the Internet for everyone to see again," Reid says, ratting out their fallen queen. I guess there really is no honor amongst thieves.

"But Reid's the one who actually did it," Tania says, trying to take some of the blame off herself. "I just took the pictures. He put it on the Web," she says. Tania still sounds a little too nonchalant for me. This girl needs the fear of God put in her, and now. Before I can do anything, Mickey lunges for her, snatching her broomstick and swinging it at her, causing everyone to go wild.

"Okay, ladies, break it up," Stan and Dan say, pulling Mickey off a stunned Tania. Nellie, looking sorrowful, holds on to Chance as she cries. I'm glad it's all out in the open now. I knew that trick was the one behind everything. What I still don't get is why Nellie didn't come to us for help. I know she wanted to be in the popular crowd, but not like this—I hope.

"Jayd, you think you're so smart!" Tania yells. She's completely lost her cool now. "Well, don't think you're going to get too far with Jeremy—or my baby daddy, as you probably refer to him. His family doesn't like brown babies, and Jeremy and his brothers know it." She smiles deviously as she tells Jeremy's family business in front of the entire school. "And all those nice gifts he buys you are out of guilt. I have a closet full of them," she adds as she and Mickey are escorted in opposite directions to cool off. I feel like my entire world's just been blown up in public.

"Jayd, are you okay?" Rah says, hugging me as he leads me away from the spectators. Nigel has followed after Mickey, and Chance and Nellie are already at the door. I guess the night's over for us. Although it was successful, I can't help but feel slightly defeated. "I'm sorry it had to go down like that," Rah says, and I know he is. No matter how much he's hurt me in the past, I don't believe he ever wants to see me suffer.

"I'm okay," I say. It's not like I'm learning anything new. I already felt most of what Tania said. Just hearing it aloud brings the pain to a whole other level. "Just a little embarrassed."

"Well, you shouldn't be," he says, leading me to sit down on a bench right outside the gym. It's a starry night, and the breeze makes me feel a little lighter. "If it's one thing I've always admired about you, Jayd, it's that you're a ride-or-die chick to whomever you call a friend, and that's never something you should be ashamed of."

"How come you're so sweet to me now that we aren't together?" I say.

"Who says we're not?" Rah says, leaning into me and kissing my lips, this time hungrier than before. "Whenever you're ready to come back, just say the word." Why is he doing this to me? Even if Jeremy and I don't work out, which if what Tania's saying is true is exactly what's going to happen, that doesn't mean I should go running back into Rah's arms.

"Hey, you two," Mickey says as she and Nigel walk up, disturbing our flow, and I'm glad. I'm too weak for this boy to fight off his kisses. "Have you seen Nellie?" She sounds worried about our girl. Now, that's the Mickey I know and love.

"She went out the other side," I say, looking around.

Everyone's still inside enjoying the party. It'll probably go on until at least one in the morning, knowing these folks, with the wild after-parties to follow.

"Well, I want a public apology from the broad for both of us," Mickey says, making all of us laugh. I'll be so glad when we're back to normal, whatever that is. It's been too weird not having my girls as friends. There are enough enemies out there to fight with. We don't need any in our little crew.

"Mickey, just be glad to have her back on our side," I say as Nellie and Chance head our way. Nellie looks weak and tired, like she's just experienced an exorcism or something.

"I'm waiting," Mickey says, not even giving Nellie an opportunity to get over here completely. I'm just glad she's giving their friendship a second chance.

"I'm really sorry," Nellie says, breaking down into fits of hard sobbing before Mickey and I embrace her, having a girl moment, with the boys looking at us, amused. "I'll do anything you want to make it up." Nellie looks both Mickey and myself in the eye.

"Anything?" Mickey asks. Oh, shit, I wonder what she has in mind.

"Anything," Nellie says, sounding like she wants to take it back but is too scared to admit it. And she'd better not take it back, because, knowing Mickey, she won't be so forgiving next time.

"You have to be me and Jayd's personal servant indefinitely, Miss Princess," Mickey says. I actually like the sound of that punishment.

"Okay," Nellie says, sounding relieved. Rah, Nigel and Chance shake their heads as we all head toward the parking lot. "And, Jayd, I'm sorry about what Tania's said about Jeremy. But unfortunately she's not lying about that. She does have a closet full of expensive gifts and cards from Jeremy while they were together." I didn't need the validation; I already knew it was true. Rah looks at me as if to say, "I told you so," but he doesn't say it. I'll deal with one nightmare at a time. Right now, I'm just happy to have my girls back in sync with each other. It'll make all the other drama in my life easier to handle, knowing my girls are cool.

"You guys want to take pictures?" Chance says, noticing the photographer is still set up with no line to wait in. Everyone else has probably already taken their photos.

"Yeah, we need a group photo to remember this shit. Plus, we still look good," Nigel says, lightening the mood. We choose the cemetery background and strike a pose for the camera, forever solidifying our victory in reality. Now, if I could just turn around my relationship with Jeremy. I don't want to give our haters the satisfaction of being right. But, unlike the fairy tales that lied to me as a little girl, all dreams aren't meant to come true.

~ 16 ~
A Gangster's Dream

"Girl, you opened my eyes/
And I'm gonna be much better for you."

—JOHN LEGEND

I've been trying to figure out how to handle Jeremy since Tania's final stab with her confession yesterday. I didn't get a chance to talk to him last night because me and my re-united crew hung out at Roscoe's Chicken and Waffles until early this morning. Rah and Nigel didn't go to their dance at Westingle and decided to kick it with us. Chance was the only one who didn't join in on clowning Nellie for being the true princess that she is.

It felt good chilling with my old crew. And with my mom out of town until tomorrow morning, I don't have to worry about beating her home tonight either, which means I can also stay out as late as I want. Her going to Vegas with Karl is me and my mom's little secret, because if Mama found out she left me alone for the weekend, she'd flip out on both of us.

"Very cute picture, but me no see the White boy in it," Sarah says in her thick Jamaican accent, snapping me out of my daydream about the dance and after-party. It's nice having a reminder of our successful evening on my key chain.

"Shut up, Sarah," I say, snatching my picture from her and returning it to my back pocket. I have yet to confront Jeremy about Tania's treasure chest, but I'll take care of that when he picks me up from work in a little while. I have a session tonight at Rah's and want to get my relationship issues squared away now. I wish Rah and I could stay together, but it seems like we're just not a good match. Although we have a lot in common, our values are different, and that's a big problem that no kiss can make disappear.

"Those jeans are so tight I'm surprised you can squeeze anything else into them," Sarah says, being her blunt self. I haven't worn this pair of Levi's in a while, and they seem to fit tighter than I remember.

"I know, girl. I'm trying to get mama hips like you, without having the baby," I say, laughing at her silly self as she struts her full-figured behind in front of me. She has a son and a baby daddy at home living with her, her mother and her older sister. Now, that's family.

"Ladies," Marty says, ruining our moment of fun. I'm glad it's almost time for me to go home, because even the sight of this trick makes my blood boil. "I think there is plenty to do around here to keep you busy without playing *America's Next Top Model* while you're supposed to be working."

"I don't know that I'd qualify for that show, being that I'm Jamerican," Sarah says, making me and Alonzo laugh. But Marty doesn't find her joke amusing at all.

"Whatever, Sarah," Marty says, joining us behind the counter and checking the register.

"I'm clocking out in twenty minutes," I say, defending my territory. No one is supposed to touch our registers while we're clocked into them—only Summer and Shahid.

"Well, I'll cash you out early. I need you to check the bathrooms before leaving. Sarah, you can empty the trash," Marty says, taking her management position too far.

"That's not my job; I'm a cashier, and I'm not letting you cash my register out. That's not the way I was taught," I say, causing my coworkers to fall silent as I defend our turf. Just because she's the only supervisor here right now doesn't mean I won't check her ass. I thought she already knew not to go there with me, but I guess some people just don't learn.

"You don't have a choice, Jayd," Marty says, pressing the ENTER key and causing the register to ring, running my receipt for the day. "It's already done. Now, the bathrooms, please." She takes my drawer to the office and shuts the door.

"Damn, why she got to be so stank all the time?" I say, pissed.

"I heard that," she says through the closed door. I really don't give a damn what she hears, because I intend to let it be heard by everyone who cares to know tomorrow. I'm going to make it clear that I won't work under her anymore, even if it means losing my job. I'd hate to let Simply Wholesome go, but I'm sure I can find another job somewhere.

"Jayd, we got you if your register comes up short or something," Alonzo says as he cuts up fresh fruit for our famous smoothies. This used to be such a fun place to work, until Marty arrived from hell only knows where. "You were right not to cash out voluntarily before your shift is up," he says as Sarah nods in agreement while she collects the trash from behind the counter before going around the store.

"And I wouldn't be cleaning no bathrooms either if I were you," Sarah continues. "That was never mentioned to me in no interview."

"I know. Where does she get off?" I ask. "Screw it. I'm clocking out. She can dock me for the fifteen minutes if she wants, but I've had enough for one day." I grab my backpack off the wall and punch my time card in the clock before walking out the front door. "See y'all tomorrow."

"Bye, Jayd," Sarah says, giving me a hug before heading to the dumpster outside. I know she doesn't mind too much because it gives her the chance to get out for a minute.

"Hey, Jayd, I heard you be hooking them braids up," Alonzo

says, catching me off guard. Rah must've told him the last time he came up here. "You think you can hook a brotha up with those Iverson rows?" He's referring to the fish-bone braids the basketball superstar made famous.

"I wish I could help you, but all I do is straight-back, gangsta style," I say. I'm not into all the fancy braids everyone's wearing nowadays, and neither is Rah, thank goodness.

"That's cool. I saw your boy's hair, and it looks fly, no shit," he says, making my spirits lift before I head out the door. Rah probably wants some fresh braids after his Afro was out last night. Maybe I can hook him up tonight at the session.

"What boy?" Jeremy says as he enters the door on my exit. What's he doing here early?

"You're early," I say, leading him out the door and away from my nosey homies. Sarah looks at me from across the near empty parking lot, smiling and shaking her head. That's my girl.

"Yeah, there wasn't any traffic today," he says, his blue eyes glistening and complimenting his curly brown hair perfectly. If he wasn't so fine, our impending breakup would be a lot easier to handle. "How was work?" We walk back toward the Mustang parked illegally in the handicap spot. Who does he think he is, the owner?

"Work was shit, and I don't want to talk about it. Jeremy, aren't you afraid of getting a ticket?" I ask as we get into his ride.

"No. Should I be?" he says, starting the engine, his loud music blaring. How come I never noticed how smug he is before now?

"Uh, yeah, I would think so, being that you're not even handicapped." It must be nice living in his world without fear of any real repercussions. I'll never use my gifts to help his undeserving ass again, and I can't respect his aloofness any longer. Enough is enough.

"Girl, you worry too much. So, why was work so bad?" Jeremy asks as we head for my mom's house.

"It was okay until our new manager tried to bust my ass for no reason," I say, still upset over Marty's bull. "She's so uptight it makes work more draining than it already is." I rub my aching legs. Standing up all day is no fun.

"Then why don't you just quit?" Jeremy says like it's no big deal. "You've been complaining about it for a while now."

"It's not that simple," I say. Even if I know I can find another job, I'm comfortable at Simply Wholesome, and I like most everything else about working there, except for Marty. Before she came along, the most annoying thing about going to work was the occasional pissy customer. But having a bitch for a boss trumps a bougie-ass patron any day. "I've been working here for over a year now, and I like it. And why should I let her win?"

"Because it's not always about winning," he says, sounding too Zen-like for me today. There's always a winner and a loser in these types of situations. And I'm not about to lose this battle.

"And sometimes it is." After an extended period of silence, Jeremy changes the subject, giving me the perfect opening for my next topic of discussion.

"I talked to Chance this morning," he says, turning down the radio. "He told me what happened at the dance." I hope that's all he told him. Chance hung out with us last night and knew I didn't want Jeremy to know about our impromptu late dinner. I hope he was a good friend to me and kept his mouth shut.

"Yeah, it was pretty ugly," I say, recalling Laura's mouthful of worms. As long as it wasn't my girl, I don't really care. I feel like everyone else got just what they deserved. Well, except for Reid. But I'll handle him another time.

"You have to be more calm, Jayd. For example, in Buddhism—" Before he can finish his statement, I go off.

"Look, Jeremy, you can follow all that peaceful bullshit if you want, but everyone's life ain't always that simple. And besides, you're Jewish, not Chinese, so why are you following after some other culture's religion? Doesn't your family have traditions of their own?" I yell loud enough so people in other cars can hear.

"Yes, but we can all learn to adapt to other ways of living if the one we're born with doesn't suit us," he says.

"Yeah, well, I did a little research of my own on your chosen way of life," I say, recalling my own limited search when he first started to school me about one of his favorite religions. I have to admit, at first I was intrigued. "And I will never adapt to a philosophy that teaches that the ultimate goal of reincarnation is to come back in the highest form, which happens to be as a man."

"There's a lot more to it than that," he says, laughing at my interpretation. "You should really look into it further. I think it could be to your benefit."

"I don't need any more benefits, fool; you ain't the county, so stop trying to give me aid all the damn time. And I'm very happy with my own cultural heritage," I say. Now I'm really boiling. If I could get out of this car and walk the rest of the way back to my mom's house, I would. But after wearing my mom's red boots last night and being on my feet all day at work, I'm too tired to get my swagger on.

"Jayd, we could all leave behind some parts of our cultures—like I do with my parents' religious hang-ups. And, from what I know of Christianity, it wasn't originated by African-Americans." What the hell? "So you should be open to other ways of thinking." Is this White boy really trying to give me a history lesson and insult me at the same time? I used to think his knowledge made him attractive. But now I see that it's more of a pompous arrogance, and that's not attractive to me at all.

"What does Christianity have to do with this conversation?" I say, taken aback by his assumption. If he only knew about the religions of my ancestors, he wouldn't be so quick to judge.

"Well, I thought because your grandfather was a preacher, you were Christian," he says, recalling one of our first "get to know each other" conversations. I never did tell him about my grandmother's work, but now I see I should've had this conversation with him a long time ago.

"No, I'm not, and neither are the women in my lineage," I say, feeling the power of my claim. Just saying the words to him makes me feel bigger than I appear.

"Well, whatever. All I'm saying is that African-Americans don't really have a religion of their own, so they have to borrow from other sources," Jeremy says, sounding like most people I know, regardless of race. This is a common misconception because of the obvious disconnect during the Middle Passage. But as our lessons teach us, our spirits never died—they just changed. "And it may do you and your lineage some good to adapt to some other ways of being. Just a suggestion," he says as we pull up to my mom's apartment. I can't believe how this conversation is going, especially when morals are the main issue on my mind.

"Jeremy, my lineage is just fine. And like all other cultures, we each have our positive and negative sides, no matter how it may look to outsiders," I say as he parks in the long driveway and turns off the engine. I told him my mom didn't want me to have any company upstairs while she's out of town, and I agree—at least, not Jeremy. I'm ready to part ways with him, and now.

"Yeah, okay. But I think you need to learn how to take it easy and not take shit so seriously all the time, you know?" he says, reclining his chair and looking me in the face.

"So I should learn how to chill like you do," I say, unbuckling my seatbelt and turning in my seat to face him head-on. I want him to see me clearly when I return the insults.

"Yep, that's right," Jeremy says, smiling. He has no idea how deep he's digging his own grave.

"So you not claiming your own child is chilling in your culture," I say, shocking the conceit right out of him.

"Jayd, not this shit again. I thought we already settled this," he says, pulling his baseball cap over his eyes.

"No, we never settled it. You bought me a purse instead, remember?" I say, rolling my neck. The neighbors peek out of their windows to see me, once again, outside with my White boyfriend. I wonder if they ever talk shit about me to my mom. If they do, she's never said anything to me about it.

"Jayd, what do you want me to do? Fight Tania for the right to raise her baby? Not going to happen," Jeremy says, unrelenting in his self-righteous attitude.

"Yes, I want you to fight for something other than your brothers," I say, remembering how heated he gets when it comes to Reid and his brothers. "How can you not want to be involved with your own baby?"

"Because it's me or the baby," he says, letting out a painful part of his lineage I know nothing about. "If I keep my name on her baby, my father will disown me, and it's not worth all that, Jayd. Now, can we please drop it?" Damn, now that's heavy. I guess it's not so easy being a trust-fund baby after all. But I still have no respect for his decision or the way he's so cool with it.

"So what about Tania's guilt gifts?" I say, moving on to the next gripe on my list. "She said you used to buy her gifts when you knew something was up and you didn't want to

deal with it, especially when it concerned your racist family."
Jeremy's olive complexion turns beet red.

"What about them?" he says, not even denying it. "I say
sorry with pretty things rather than words. You act like you
don't get to benefit from it, too." Now, see, that's the arro-
gant shit I'm talking about. This fool's too much for me.

"You know what, Jeremy, where you come from, that may
be okay," I say, picking up my backpack from the car floor,
ready for a hot shower and nap before my long night. This
conversation is over, just like our relationship. "But where I
come from, that's called bribery, and I'm not for sale."

"Who's trying to buy you?" he says, sitting straight up in
his seat as I open the passenger door, ready to exit his car for
what will probably be the last time.

"You are. And you not seeing that is what makes this relationship impossible to maintain."

"So, that's it? You're breaking up with me because I buy
you nice things like this purse you were salivating over last
weekend?" he says, reaching in the backseat and pulling out
the Lucky bag that won't go away. "What am I going to do
with this?" He stretches it toward me.

"That's not my problem. And it's the reason behind the
buying, not the action itself," I say, touching the soft leather.
"I told you to return it."

"I don't return things, Jayd. Besides, it was a gift, and you
can't give gifts back," he says, lifting my chin with the gentlest
touch. He kisses me softly, but I'm still too hot to buy into his
game.

"And I can't take back my feelings, Jeremy. I'm sorry, I wish
I could say that all this doesn't matter, but it does. I can never
get over the fact that your family is classist or racist or whatever they are and that you're to chill to really give a damn," I
say, finally getting out of the car.

"Jayd, don't do this. I love you, girl. Get back in the car," Jeremy says, still not believing it's over.

"Jeremy, I need some space," I say, trying to let him down as easily as I can without crippling his pride. If I know one thing about dudes it's that they don't like to show when they're hurting. And this is one of those times for Jeremy.

"Okay, I'll check on you later, Lady J. And don't forget your bag," he says, handing me the purse through the open window before starting the car and taking off. I admit, it was fun while it lasted. But like all things, whether good or bad, they must eventually come to an end. As I walk up the stairs leading to my mom's door, my phone rings. It's Mickey.

"What up, girl? Me and Nellie are going to roll out around nine to pick you up," she says. I'm so glad to hear her say Nellie's name without any hate in her voice.

"Cool," I say, sounding as exhausted as my body feels.

"Is everything okay, girl?" Nellie says, chiming in on the three-way call. "You sound awful." It's been a long day, and I need to wind down.

"Jeremy and I just broke up," I say, realizing for the first time it's true. Breakups never feel good, even if they are the only option left in a mismatched relationship like ours.

"Well, it's about time," Mickey says, not hiding her joy. "Now, we can get down to business and get you and Rah back together?"

"Whatever, Mickey. I'll see y'all later," I say, ignoring her jovial disposition.

"I'm sorry about you and Jeremy, Jayd," Nellie says, sounding truly sympathetic.

"I know you really like each other."

"Yeah, but that isn't always enough," I say, stating the obvious. If relationships were that easy, no one would ever break up.

"We'll catch up with you in a few hours, Jayd. And wear those red boots again. I think Rah likes them."

"What are you, my pimp now?" I say to Mickey as she and Nellie hang up, leaving me to my mom's peaceful apartment. I need some space before we go out tonight. It feels good to be alone for a change, even if it's only temporary.

"Where are the boots?" Mickey says as she and Nellie pull up the driveway, bumping Mary J, who's singing my exact sentiments about Jeremy. I wasn't thinking straight to think we were ever meant to be.

"I wanted to chill," I say. I opted for my black Old Navy roll-up cargo pants and a pink top with some sneakers. Casual is how I'm feeling about everything in my life at this moment. I performed a miniature head cleansing on myself during my shower. I read in Maman's stories about cleansing after separations. And I do feel much lighter than I did a few hours ago. I'm also glad my girls are here and we're going to hang out with my boys. Life is still good, with or without a boyfriend.

"There's chilling, and then there's just not caring," Mickey says, gesturing toward her body, which displays her gold jacket and belt, with the high mules to match. Her jeans are much tighter than the ones I wore to work today, and I'm sure Nigel will find her outfit very appealing. "Girl, if you're going to get Rah back, you've got to step it up a notch. Them heffas at Westingle don't play when it comes to gear." Mickey's right, but I've never been one to care about what the status quo is wearing or doing. And it's time for that side of Jayd to come out more. This entire school year has been about what other people think, but that's over. It's time for people to know the real me and for me to stop second-guessing myself.

"Jayd doesn't care what those girls are wearing. She's

prettier and smarter than all of them combined," Nellie says, looking the preppiest of us all in her capri pants and form-fitting top. She still looks thin, but her color's coming back, and she looks happier than I've seen her since she got that godforsaken crown.

"Well, thank you, Nellie," I say, just happy to climb into the backseat of the Regal behind my girls. "And for the record, Mickey, I'm not trying to get Rah back. I'm actually feeling good about not having a man right now."

"Is that right?" Mickey says, sounding unconvinced. "So that's why you're now sporting the same purse that you just broke up with your ex-man over."

"Let's just say it was a little parting gift. Besides, you're right—I did earn this bag," I say, giving me and my girls a good laugh. And with my job on the line, I don't know when I'll be able to afford a nice bag like this one. If Jeremy wants to give it to me, I'll take it, especially now that we're not to-gether. At least he now knows that bribes don't always work to his advantage.

"I hear you, girl. But I still think you should give Rah an-other shot. He really loves you," Mickey says as we pull up behind Nigel's Impala. Rah's Acura isn't in the driveway; he must've stepped out.

"Jayd," Kamal says as we walk up the side path toward the back door of the garage turned studio. "I'm so glad you're here."

"I'm glad to see you, too, little man," I say, kissing him on the head.

"Hi, Nellie and Mickey. Rah went to the store. He'll be right back, but Nigel and Chance are kicking it already," Kamal says.

"Well, aren't you a good little host," I say as we follow him inside.

"Now we can get this party started," Nigel says, changing

the music from some of their beats to Peaches & Herb's "Reunited."

"Nigga, you crazy," Mickey says, kissing her man and landing in his lap on the sofa next to Chance. Nigel's eyes look pleased at her outfit, just as I anticipated.

"Hey, Chance," Nellie says, overly enthusiastic to see him. Maybe after all she's been through with Tania, and with Chance by her side during it all, she's starting to value him for the real friend he is in her life and not just someone to use. She takes a seat next to him on the couch as he nods "what's up" to me. With everyone coupled off, I take a seat at Rah's desk and look around at my friends. Although we have our problems, I wouldn't want to be anywhere else.

"Rah, it's about time you got back," Nigel says, looking toward the back door. As he walks into the room headed straight for me, my heart begins to beat so fast I swear it's going to leap out of my chest.

"What's up, everyone?" Rah says as he picks up the remote controlling our soundtrack. "I want y'all to hear some new shit we came up with this afternoon." He smiles at me and kisses me with his eyes.

"Yeah, Jayd, I know you're going to love it," Nigel says. He and Mickey are smiling so big I know something's up. The melodic bass line gets us all in a chill mood before they even start rolling their blunts and sipping their drinks. Rah has mad skills in the studio.

"Where are the words?" Nellie says, stating the obvious as Chance starts the session by taking the first puff.

"All we've got is the hook so far. Here it comes," Rah says, turning the volume up. "The title is 'A Gangster's Dream.' " As the beat continues, Nigel's hypnotic voice raps the hook, "You might be a weak boy's nightmare, but you're a gangster's dream," for Rah's new beat, and I'm speechless as everyone looks at me and then Rah, awaiting our responses.

"I don't mean to talk about your boy," Nigel says, accepting Chance's pass before continuing, "but that White boy was stupid if he thought there was something wrong with you, Jayd."

"Nigel's right," Chance says, finally stepping up and being the big brother I've always known him to be. "Jeremy isn't good enough for you, and I love him like a brother."

"Yeah, but you already knew that, didn't you, queen," Rah says, taking me by the hand as he kneels in front of me. "You're too strong for him but just right for me." He kisses my hands and sits down on the floor in between my legs before handing me the small paper bag holding a Snickers bar and black rubber bands for his hair. As I massage his scalp before braiding his thick crown, I know this feels too good to be temporary. However this reality plays itself out, I'm down for the ride.

Epilogue

With my mom still gone for the night, I decided to fall asleep on Rah's fold-out couch with the rest of my crew. As tired as I am, I still can't get any restful sleep. Luckily I've decided to go into work late, so I can sleep in a little longer if need be. Just as I fall into a semi-peaceful slumber, my dream begins, and it's anything but serene.

The shiny black Monte Carlo pulls up alongside the football field, causing the few people in the bleachers to take notice of the classic vehicle tweaked out with limo tint. The license plate reads G 4 LIFE, *and I know it's my girl's man without the confirmation apparent on her petrified face. What's Mickey's boyfriend doing at football practice? He's never been up here before, not even to escort her to a dance, not that she usually goes to them all. This can't be good.*

When Nigel and the other players return from their water break, the windows on the almost cloaked vehicle open, and someone starts to shout out at Nigel.

"Nigel!" Mickey shouts, but not before her man steps out of the vehicle and rushes to the field with two other dudes right behind him. Mickey runs onto the field from where we're seated on the sidelines, and I follow with Nellie and

Chance right behind us. Unfortunately Rah's nowhere in sight, and we're no match for Mickey's man and his crew.

"Jayd, you still going to work?" Rah says, whispering in my ear as the rest of our friends still sleep. We've been lying here for hours.

"Yeah," I whisper back. Should I tell him about my dream right now?

"I'll take you back to your mom's and then to work whenever you're ready," he says, falling back into place next to me on the crowded bed. What am I going to do about Mickey's man snatching Nigel up at school?

Remember what I told you, Jayd: separate your emotions from your visions. Then you'll be able to master your powers, my mom says. She must not be having a very good time in Vegas if she's got time to be all up in my head.

I always have time for my baby, she says, still here. I've got a lot of work to do on myself. And, even with Rah back in my life, he doesn't need to be my man. Not yet, anyway. It's time for some me time, and I'm ready to claim my powerful heritage fully—fiery attitude, drama and all. And I must do it alone, for now.

Drama High, Volume 4:
FRENEMIES

L. Divine

ABOUT THIS GUIDE

The following questions are intended to
enhance your group's reading of
DRAMA HIGH: FRENEMIES
by L. Divine.

DISCUSSION QUESTIONS

1. Who is Rah to Jayd? How has his presence affected Jayd's life? Is his influence a positive, negative, or both?

2. Is Mickey being a good friend to Nellie or is she jealous, as Nellie accuses? How does Jayd deal with her friends being at war?

3. How has Nellie's crown changed her behavior and the way that people respond to her? What is it about Nellie's attitude that irritates both Jayd and Mickey?

4. How does Jayd bargain her way out of a day of A.P. meetings? Does Jayd benefit from being in the A.P. program?

5. How did Jayd find out about Tania's pregnancy and that Jeremy's the father? What was her initial reaction to the news?

6. How have Lynn Marie's powers affected her and Jayd's relationship? Do you think it's an invasion of privacy? If so, is this a good thing?

7. What did Jayd do to help her friends? Did her actions work as she had expected?

8. How does Jeremy's father feel about black women? What would happen to the Weiner boys, Jeremy in particular, if they were to have babies with their current girlfriends?

9. Is Jeremy's love for Jayd real? Is the love that Jayd feels for Jeremy equal to the love she feels for Rah?

10. Why does Jeremy's comment about black religion bother Jayd so much? Do you agree with his comment?

11. How do Mama and their spiritual lineage influence Jayd's everyday life?

12. What was the breaking point that ended Jeremy and Jayd's relationship? Do you think they should try and work it out or stay separated for good?

13. What was the hook for Rah's latest beat? Why do you think he wrote these lyrics for Jayd?

Stay tuned for the next book
in the DRAMA HIGH series
LADY J

Until then, satisfy your DRAMA HIGH craving
with the following excerpt from
the next exciting installment.

ENJOY!

Prologue

After my dream this morning about Mickey's man jumping Nigel, I never did get back to sleep. Rah made me breakfast and took me home to get dressed before taking me to work this morning. He's such a sweety. But the sweetness ended when he started to get repeat text messages and calls from his girl Trina, snapping me into the reality of the situation: if I want to be with Rah, I'll have to deal with being the other woman always, because I don't see him changing his ways anytime soon. I respect his Muslim culture, but I ain't down with the multiple wives thang. That reality doesn't suit me at all.

Thank goodness my mom's picking me up from work in a few minutes. I've never been so tired in my life, not even when Mama keeps me up all night working in the spirit room. I think it's my job wearing me down. I'm starting to feel like the people I see going to work on the bus every day: miserable.

"So how was your trip?" I ask as my mom pulls off the curb towards Inglewood. She decided to pick me up from work so she can get me back to Mama's early. I guess her and Carl have a followup to their Vegas date later this evening. Girls in

general are a trip when they get a new man. And my mom's
no exception to the rule.

"It was wonderful," my mom says, her green eyes sparkling
over her Versace shades. They must be a gift from her new
man because I know they're not in her budget. "But the
date's not over yet. We're going to The Cheesecake Factory
for dinner, so you've got ten minutes to get your stuff when
we get back, okay? I'll wait for you downstairs." Damn, it's
like that? It seems like second nature for women to put a guy
as top priority when he's around. That's exactly why, no matter how much I may love Rah, I've decided not to have a man
right now. Who needs the drama?

*"I do, and so does every other woman I know including
you, little miss thang,"* my mom says telepathically. I hate
when she does that.

*"If you don't like it, then speak what's on your mind,
shawty,"* she says, again without moving her lips.

"Okay then fine," I say, still vexed from having to work
under Marty again today. I have to find a new job and soon.
"How come every time a new dude pops up I become second in line?" I say, feeling the pain of my words knot in my
throat. Whenever I get emotional I want to cry. My mom sees
it as a sign of weakness, so I try not to let it happen too often
in front of her and this time is no exception.

"You're never second, Jayd," my mom says, as she speeds
down La Brea like it's the Autobahn. "But, between work and
you on the weekends, I never have enough time to just be
me," she says, sounding like the self-absorbed Lynn Marie
that Mama always talks about. From the time I could remember, which has been basically all of my life, Mama has called
my mother selfish and materialistic without hesitation. I used
to defend my mother until I got a little older and understood
that Mama was telling the truth; otherwise my mom would
have raised me herself. I try not to blame her too much. Al-

though it's times like these that make me rethink my forgiving attitude.

"Oh Jayd, I know you think I'm selfish and you're right," she says, turning onto her street and unlocking the doors before stopping the car. "But honestly, Jayd, you've been able to take care of yourself since you were very young. When you get older you'll appreciate having such an independent mother. No matter how Mama may feel about it, I know you came to me because you knew who I was before we met. I used to talk to you in the womb all of the time and you responded. I know you heard me, so don't act like this is news," she says, touching my hand and looking into my eyes. If it weren't for their colors, our eyes would be identical.

"I know Mom, I know," I say, opening the car door and exiting before she makes me cry. I can actually remember having dreams about talking to my mother from inside of her belly. Mama says it's typical for me and other babies born with cauls to have memories revealed through dreams, even into our past lives. Caught up in my thoughts, I trip on the curb, splashing the murky drain water onto my Nikes and accidentally causing the car door to get stuck on the sidewalk.

"Okay, then. So don't be so salty when I want to go out. It's all for you baby. And be careful with that door," she says, forcing a sarcastic smirk across my face. My mom's nothing if not honest about who she is, and I definitely admire her for that. With or without a king-man, my mom's a queen. And I, being her daughter, wear a similar crown and deserve more than what any of these dudes around here are offering me now. I know I can do better on my own and that's just what I intend to do.

~ 1 ~
Cruise Control

"I'm not here for your entertainment/
You don't really want to mess with me."

—PINK

I don't mind being back on the bus and hiking the near mile it takes to get to school every morning. The brisk morning air feels refreshing against my cheeks. I can tell my legs have become a little weak from the daily rides with Jeremy. But, I doubt I'll still receive that privilege now that we're no longer an item. I feel awful about our breakup. I do still have feelings for him, but not as strong as I do for Rah. Speaking of which, here's a text from him now. I'll hit him back later. Right now I want to mentally prepare for my day while hiking up this steep-ass hill—no distractions allowed.

As the procession of fancy cars passes me up toward South Bay High, I notice Misty walking up ahead of me on the other side of the street. I guess her mom's running late this morning and couldn't give her a ride, which isn't that unusual. I saw her on the three bus rides it takes to get here, but luckily they were all packed as usual, forcing a safe distance between us.

I'm still surprised Misty couldn't catch a ride with someone else from South Central. I guess she wanted to roll solo this morning, too. But it's odd for Misty to ride alone, unlike myself. I actually prefer the solitude I find on the bus; it gives me time to think. Mama says I should use this time to study

my lessons, and I do for the most part. But, instead of reading or writing them down, I recite what I already know in my
head. It's hard enough to concentrate on these noisy and
bumpy rides as it is. Besides, I don't like to have too much in
my hands just in case I got to make a quick move. You never
know when the driver will pass up a stop or a fight will break
out. I'm always on my toes.

When I finally arrive on campus, Chance is waiting for me
by my locker with Nellie and Mickey, of course. I must admit,
I love having my crew back together. This weekend's chill
session was just what we needed to get our groove back.
And, spending time with Rah is always cool, especially when
we're in the studio. His new song still has me blushing, but
not blind to the painful facts. Rah has a girl and I am single.
I've had three relationships in four months and it's time for
me to chill. I'm letting time take over for now, leaving the
controls on cruise while I sit back and enjoy the ride.

"Hey y'all," I say, interrupting what looks like a deep conversation. "What's up?"

"Hey Jayd," Nellie says, putting her lean arm around my
shoulders and escorting me to my locker. What's her problem? "How are you feeling, girl," she says as I open my locker
door, retrieving my Spanish and English books for my first two
periods. I haven't forgotten them in my locker for the past couple of weeks and I have to admit, I'm proud of my progress.

"I'm feeling fine, Nellie. Are you okay?" I say, putting my
hand on her forehead, checking for a fever.

"Girl, stop playing," she says, slapping my hand away from
her face and taking a step back towards Chance and Mickey,
who are amused at our behavior. They look just as concerned as she does.

"Nellie's just making sure you're okay. This is the first day
back since you and Jeremy broke up," Mickey says, taking her
watermelon Blow Pop out of her mouth long enough to

translate Nellie's body language. "Everyone's already talking about it."

"Yeah, it's pretty brutal," Chance says, grabbing Nellie by the waist like she's his property to claim. This blossoming relationship should be the talk of the town, not my breakup with Jeremy.

"Is there something I should know about you two?" I say, slamming my locker shut and leading the way out of the busy hall. I do notice people I don't even know looking at me and whispering to their friends. Bad news travels fast, especially when it's about the most popular cat in school and his chocolate pick of the month.

"Yeah, you should know that people are cashing in on their bets of how long you and Jeremy would last," Chance says, looking towards South Central, where Misty has joined in the crowd. I'm sure she's having a field day with this one. I'm surprised she didn't say anything on the bus. But, from the looks of it, she had more important things on her mind. I'm still confused as to why KJ didn't give her a ride. Aren't they still dating?

"Yeah, it's pretty pathetic what some people will bet five dollars on," Mickey says, looking directly at Shae. I can't say I'm surprised. Jeremy is the most popular cat at this wack-ass school and his life is of public interest.

"Only five dollars? I'm worth way more than that," I say, making light of the humiliating situation while giving my friends a good laugh.

"Yes you are," Chance says, letting go of Nellie long enough to give me a bear hug. "None of these dudes up here are good enough for my girl," he says, making Nellie feel slightly uncomfortable by the looks of it. Here we go. I don't like the idea of my best friends dating, especially not when Chance used to have a crush on me. Even though nothing went down between us, I know how females are when it comes to their men, even my girls. Mickey would have had beef with me

if Nigel and I used to date. And, I know it bothers Nellie that
Chance used to have it bad for me. But now he's hooked on
her and I hope she concentrates on the future and not the past.

"Yeah girl, you already got your man," Mickey says, referring to Rah. "You just need to woman up and fight for the
fool," she says, now loudly smacking her candy-turned-gum
as the first bell rings.

"Nobody needs to woman up, Foxy Brown," I say, teasing
my girl who's still wearing the attitude of her Halloween costume. I'm glad we took pictures of that night; we all looked
good. Noticing me eye my key chain before securing it into
one of the many pockets on my Jansport, Nellie takes hers
out and clasps it to her backpack.

"Hey, let's all wear our pictures on our bags," she says,
taking Chance's key chain and hooking it onto his backpack.

"What are we, in junior high?" Mickey says. Before she can
protest any further, Nellie takes Mickey's out of her purse
and locks it to her backpack as well.

"No. But we can still show love, right, Jayd," she says,
waiting for me to follow suit. I take the picture off of my clut-
tered key chain and move it to my backpack, next to the "No
More Drama" satchel Mama gave me for the first day of school.

"Are you happy?" I say, sassing Nellie as we continue to move
toward our classes. "Now we officially look like the clique I
never wanted to be a part of."

"There's a big difference between our crew and those
other cliques," Nellie says, putting one arm around me and
another around Mickey's shoulders, forcing Chance to again
release her waist.

"What's that?" Mickey says, dryly. Mickey's not into belong-
ing with any one set of folks, or any one dude for that matter.
I know she and her man have been together since junior high,
but I doubt that she's ever been exclusive. And, according to my
dream Saturday night, her unfaithful shit's about to hit the fan.

"We're real friends; ride or die." As Nellie says something that sounds more like Mickey's mantra, I see KJ and his crew looking my way. He has a big smile on his face, so I know he must be talking about me and Jeremy's breakup. I wonder if Jeremy's getting this kind of heat on the white side of Drama High.

"Yeah, whatever," Mickey says. "Let's just try to stay on the right side of our friendship from now on." I couldn't agree more; we've already had enough drama for the year, and we're only in the second month of school. But I doubt it will seriously happen. If I know one thing about our crew, it's that we have haters. And where there are haters, there's always drama.

"There's the final bell," Chance says, pulling Nellie off toward first period as I head toward my Spanish class.

"Alright. I'll see y'all at lunch. I have to talk to my English teacher at break," I say. Mrs. Malone's helping me go over my last paper. She thinks I didn't try hard enough and wants me to revise it for an A. I wish all of my teachers were cool like her. Most of them would just let my little black self fail.

"Damn Jayd. School isn't all about work," Nellie says, allowing Chance to lead her away from me.

"If I didn't know better, I'd say you loved this wicked-ass place," Mickey says, following the new couple away from the quad.

"Bye y'all. And don't make any more bets on my relationships," I yell after them. I know they didn't, but I'm sure the thought crossed both of their minds.

"Hey Jayd. What's up with my girl?" Nigel says as he swoops me up into a huge hug, walking me out of my classroom as I head in, catching me off-guard. He must've had a meeting with his coach, who also doubles as my Spanish teacher. Thank God I'm not trying to take the AP exam in this subject because I'd fail from his inadequate teaching for sure.

"Nothing much. Aren't you going to be late for class?" I say as he puts my Nikes back on the ground.

"I'm an athlete baby," he says, showing off his hall pass from Mr. Donald. "We're always excused."

"Whatever Nigel," I say, pushing the heavy door out of his hands and passing him up. As I enter the classroom, I notice a new girl is sitting in my seat. She looks a little shaken so I'm not going to sweat her today. I'll just have to be here a little early tomorrow morning to stake my claim.

"Have you talked to my boy this morning?" he says, escorting me to my temporary desk as the rest of the class makes their way into the chilly room. First period's always the coolest. I don't know if it's because of the morning frost or the air conditioning they use to keep us awake, but I'm always glad to get out of this room.

"No, but he texted me a little while ago. I've just been too preoccupied to hit him back," I say, only telling half the truth. Ever since his girl started texting while we were together yesterday, I've been rethinking just how attached I want to get with Rah right now. I'm just glad he's not at my school everyday. He would be too irresistible for me to think twice about getting back with him if he were up in my face all of the time. Being at South Bay High does have its advantages.

"Well, you know he doesn't like to be kept waiting," Nigel says, grinning and showing off his bright smile. Mickey doesn't have a chance against falling hard for Nigel. I just have to help all of us not get hurt by the heat their forbidden love is stirring up.

"Yeah, I remember well. And you will both remember that I don't play games," I say, taking my seat as Mr. McDonald writes today's agenda on the board.

"Yeah, whatever Jayd. You're a trip. Just hit him back," Nigel says, finally leaving the room and me to my thoughts. I can't handle Rah and my first day broken up with Jeremy at the same time. I'm not looking forward to third period. I know Tania's got to be glowing over the news of us breaking up. I just hope she doesn't say anything to set me off because the last thing I need is more heat in my fire this morning.

After first period, second period was a breeze because we watched *The Color Purple* in class, comparing it to the novel, which we read last week. I love Mrs. Malone's book list. She makes the best selections and also the most diverse. Our summer reading list included works from Sandra Cisneros, Zora Neale Hurston and Julie Dash. I don't know if any of those authors will be on the AP exam for sure, but I enjoyed reading them anyway.

"Can I just rewrite my paper on Alice Walker's literary voice rather than Virginia Woolf's," I ask, whining about my last assignment. I hated reading *A Room of One's Own*. Not because Woolf's writing sucks, but because I don't like her style. It just doesn't speak to me. And that's exactly what I tried to express in my paper.

"I like your critique of Ms. Woolf's voice," Mrs. Malone says, propping herself up onto the desk in front of mine, displaying her cream and turquoise moccasins. She looks like she just stepped out of a New Mexican tourist guide's brochure. "You just need a more solid argument," she says, handing me a paper heavily marked in red. Damn, that means hella work on my end.

"It doesn't look like you liked much about it," I say, flipping each of the five pages, revealing more red ink as I go along. It looks like she bled all over it.

"Jayd, all of these notes aren't bad. Don't always expect the worst," she says, leaning over and turning to the third page. "Take for example this page. I wrote a paragraph explaining how this is where your actual thesis begins instead of being on page one, which is where it belongs. This is your rough draft, Jayd. Turn in the final one to me by Friday," Mrs. Malone says, closing the paper and placing it on the desk in front of me. "I've seen you do much better. But you've seemed a little distracted lately. Everything okay at home?"

"Yes, everything's fine," I say, looking at her wall clock, ready to roll. There are only five more minutes left in break and I really could use a Snickers right now. Mrs. Malone's always looking for some after school special type of conversation with me. She's cool, but I'd never tell her all of my business. Mama would hang me where I stand if I ever told any of my teachers about my home life. I learned that lesson very early when I was in elementary school.

"Is everything okay with Jeremy?" she says, like we're old girlfriends having tea. Ah, hell nah, let me nip this one in the bud right now.

"Jeremy's no longer my concern," I say, rising from my seat, wounded report in hand. "I'll have the paper back to you by Friday and thank you again for letting me rewrite it," I say, marching toward the door. Damn, there's the first bell. Now I'm going to have to go to third period without my chocolate fix. I really hope everything's cool with both Jeremy and Tania. Any more irritation and I'm liable to bite someone's head off.

"Jayd, if you ever need to talk, I'm here. I know breaking up seems like the end of the world, but it's only high school," she says, whimsically dismissing my feelings as a school girl crush. Even with Rah winning the battle for my heart, I still feel for Jeremy.

"Thank you, Mrs. Malone," I say as I walk toward third period. Right now I just feel out of control of my feelings, like they're marching to their own beat and I'm along for the ride.

"*The key is to be in alignment with your feelings in order to control the situation*," my mom says, sounding more like Mama than herself as she invades my thoughts.

"Not at school," I say aloud to my mom as she coquettishly grins in my head. She's having too much fun with her born-again powers. But, I know she's right. I have to get my mojo back, as Netta would say, and fast.

"Hey Jayd," Jeremy says, walking into our class right as the bell rings and taking the seat next to me, as usual. I guess some things haven't changed.

"Hey," I say, unable to muster anything else. I'm still so upset with him for not claiming his and Tania's baby because he's afraid of his dad disowning him, but I also feel guilty because it was an easy way out for me to be free to explore something new with Rah. But Jeremy doesn't have to know all that.

"Good morning class," Mrs. Peterson says, barely looking up from her desk. "Your assignment's on the board. Your quiz will be at the last fifteen minutes of the period. If you must talk, make it quiet please." Before returning to her newspaper, Mrs. Peterson looks up at the opening door ready to attack whoever's walking into her arena late. "Thank you for joining us this morning," she says a hella salty to a tardy Tania.

"Well, it's the least I can do, considering it's my last morning at South Bay," Tania says, sliding an envelope across the teacher's desk, as giddy as ever. She turns around to wink at Jeremy while giving me a sly look. She then walks to the back of the classroom to where her followers are seated and collects money while Mrs. Peterson signs her release papers. I know this trick didn't place a bet on me and Jeremy.

"Jeremy," she says, leaning across my desk, right in striking distance. "It's been real," she says, blowing him a kiss as she cuts her eyes at me. "And, so sorry the two of you didn't work out," she says, showing off her fifty-dollar bill and blinging engagement ring, before walking back toward Mrs. Peterson's desk. The broad's lucky she's pregnant. Otherwise, whipping her ass might be worth the automatic suspension from school.

"What a bitch," Jeremy says under his breath, but loud enough to make the students around us giggle. Well, at least Jeremy and I are in agreement about something.

"Yeah, I think our breakup is worth a whole lot more. At least a c-note," I say, breaking the iceberg between us. I would love it if we could still be friends. I genuinely like the cat and love vibing with him.

"I agree. At least a hundred. I wish they'd let me in on the bet. I could have made a killing," he says, taking his books out of his backpack and turning to our assignment. With Tania's grand exit over, it's back to work in Government class.

"I hear you. What would you have wagered?" I ask, copying the notes from the board into my notebook. I miss going back and forth with Jeremy. We seemed to lose our spark amidst all of the relationship baggage. It's nice to be on the path to friendship again, even if it's still awkward. Like Mama says, time heals all wounds or makes you forget what you were fighting about in the first place.

"A million dollars," he says, looking as serious as a heart attack, catching me off guard, much like Nigel did earlier. "I would've bet that much that we'd stay together, if the situation and timing was different." I now realize Jeremy feels as bad as I do about us breaking up. The difference between us is that he has no one to catch his rebound. My phone vibrates with another message from Rah, making me blush. Damn, this sucks. Now I really feel uncomfortable.

"Quiet please," Mrs. Peterson says, ending the heat for now. I hope Jeremy and I can really be friends, even if he does find out about me and Rah. But for now, I just pray that we can all chill for a minute before crashing head-on into each other.

START YOUR OWN BOOK CLUB

Courtesy of the DRAMA HIGH series

ABOUT THIS GUIDE

The following is intended to help you get
the Book Club you've always wanted
up and running!
Enjoy!

Start Your Own Book Club

A Book Club is not only a great way to make friends, but it is also a fun and safe environment for you to express your views and opinions on everything from fashion to teen pregnancy. A Teen Book Club can also become a forum or venue to air grievances and plan remedies for problems.

The People

To start, all you need is yourself and at least one other person. There's no criteria for who this person or persons should be other than having a desire to read and a commitment to discuss things during a certain time frame.

The Rules

Just as in Jayd's life, sometimes even Book Club discussions can be filled with much drama. People tend to disagree with each other, cut each other off when speaking, and take criticism personally. So, there should be some ground rules:

1. Do not attack people for their ideas or opinions.
2. When you disagree with a book club member on a point, disagree respectfully. This means that you do not denigrate other people for their ideas or even their ideas, themselves, i.e., no name calling or saying, "That's stupid!" Instead, say, "I can respect your position, however, I feel differently."
3. Back up your opinions with concrete evidence, either from the book in question or life in general.
4. Allow every one a turn to comment.
5. Do not cut a member off when the person is speaking. Respectfully wait your turn.
6. Critique only the idea (and do so responsibly; saying, "That's stupid!" is not allowed). Do not criticize the person.

7. Every member must agree to and abide by the ground rules.

Feel free to add any other ground rules you think might be necessary.

The Meeting Place

Once you've decided on members, and agreed to the ground rules, you should decide on a place to meet. This could be the local library, the school library, your favorite restaurant, a bookstore, or a member's home. Remember, though, if you decide to hold your sessions at a member's home, the location should rotate to another member's home for the next session. It's also polite for guests to bring treats when attending a Book Club meeting at a member's home. If you choose to hold your meetings in a public place, always remember to ask the permission of the librarian or store manager. If you decide to hold your meetings in a local bookstore, ask the manager to post a flyer in the window announcing the Book Club to attract more members if you so desire.

Timing is Everything

Teenagers of today are all much busier than teenagers of the past. You're probably thinking, "Between chorus rehearsals, the Drama Club, and oh yeah, my job, when will I ever have time to read another book that doesn't feature Romeo and Juliet!" Well, there's always time, if it's time well-planned and time planned ahead. You and your Book Club can decide to meet as often or as little as is appropriate for your bustling schedules. *Once a month* is a favorite option. *Sleepover Book Club* meetings—if you're open to excluding one gender—is also a favorite option. And in this day of high-tech, savvy teens, *Internet Discussion Groups* are also an appealing option. Just choose what's right for you!

Well, you've got the people, the ground rules, the place, and the time. All you need now is a book!

The Book

Choosing a book is the most fun. FRENEMIES is of course an excellent choice, and since it's a series, you won't soon run out of books to read and discuss. Your Book Club can also have comparative discussions as you compare the first book, THE FIGHT, to the second, SECOND CHANCE, and so on.

But depending upon your reading appetite, you may want to veer outside of the Drama High series. That's okay. There are plenty of options, many of which you will be able to find under the Dafina Books for Young Readers Program in the coming months.

But don't be afraid to mix it up. Nonfiction is just as good as fiction and a fun way to learn about from where we came without just using a history text book. Science fiction and fantasy can be fun, too!

And always, always research the author. You might find the author has a website where you can post your Book Club's questions or comments. The author may even have an e-mail address available so you can correspond directly. Authors will also sit in on your Book Club meetings, either in person, or on the phone, and this can be a fun way to discuss the book as well!

The Discussion

Every good Book Club discussion starts with questions. FRENEMIES, as will every book in the Drama High series, comes with a Reading Group Guide for your convenience, though of course, it's fine to make up your own. Here are some sample questions to get started:

1. What's this book all about anyway?
2. Who are the characters? Do we like them? Do they remind us of real people?
3. Was the story interesting? Were real issues of concern to you examined?
4. Were there details that didn't quite work for you or ring true?
5. Did the author create a believable environment—one that you could visualize?
6. Was the ending satisfying?
7. Would you read another book from this author?

Record Keeper

It's generally a good idea to have someone keep track of the books you read. Often libraries and schools will hold reading drives where you're rewarded for having read a certain number of books in a certain time period. Perhaps, a pizza party awaits!

Get Your Teachers and Parents Involved

Teachers and Parents love it when kids get together and read. So involve your teachers and parents. Your Book Club may read a particular book where it would help to have an adult's perspective as part of the discussion. Teachers may also be able to include what you're doing as a Book Club in the classroom curriculum. That way books you love to read such as the Drama High ones can find a place in your classroom alongside the books you don't love to read so much.

Resources

To find some new favorite writers, check out the following resources. Happy reading!

Young Adult Library Services Association
http://www.ala.org/ala/yalsa/yalsa.htm

Carnegie Library of Pittsburgh
Hip-Hop!
Teen Rap Titles
http://www.carnegielibrary.org/teens/read/booklists/teen rap.html

TeensPoint.org
What Teens Are Reading
http://www.teenspoint.org/reading_matters/book_list.asp?s ort=5&list=274

Teenreads.com
http://www.teenreads.com/

Sacramento Public Library
Fantasy Reading for Kids
http://www.saclibrary.org/teens/fantasy.html

Book Divas
http://www.bookdivas.com/

Meg Cabot Book Club
http://www.megcabotbookclub.com/